"D'you ride? Horses."

"It's been a while, but yeah."

"Good. I've got horses that need to be ridden. We'll take the boy with us. Day after tomorrow," he added as an afterthought, then stomped out of the kitchen.

Winnie realized how monumental this was. Except…

She turned to follow him. She found him on the back deck.

"Back where I come from," she said, "it's the custom to *ask* a woman if she'd like to do something. So—" she crossed her arms "—care to try this again?"

Aidan looked back out toward the setting sun. "I'm thinking of going horseback riding on Saturday. Wouldya be interested in goin' along?"

"I'd love to," she said, then turned smartly on her heel and walked away.

Dear Reader,

Like most writers, I find the germs for story ideas everywhere. In the case of *A Mother's Wish,* knowing several people who were adopted as infants led me to wondering about what goes through a birth mother's mind, not only when she makes that heart-wrenching decision to let someone else raise her child, but years later, as well. What if, even though you knew you'd made the right decision, you had a much harder time coming to terms with it than you expected?

And what would you do if you discovered that some tragedy had rocked the "perfect" life you'd envisioned for your child?

Join Winnie Porter as she embarks on an emotional journey with far more forks in the road than she imagined when she set out to simply catch a glimpse of the son she gave up nine years before. She discovers that the sweetest happy endings are the ones you had no idea were even possible.

Karen

A MOTHER'S WISH

KAREN TEMPLETON

Silhouette

SPECIAL EDITION®

Published by Silhouette Books

America's Publisher of Contemporary Romance

SILHOUETTE BOOKS

ISBN-13: 978-0-373-24916-9
ISBN-10:   0-373-24916-0

A MOTHER'S WISH

Visit Silhouette Books at www.eHarlequin.com

Printed in U.S.A.

Books by Karen Templeton

Silhouette Special Edition

Marriage, Interrupted #1721
††*Baby Steps* #1798
††*The Prodigal Valentine* #1808
††*Pride and Pregnancy* #1821
‡*Dear Santa* #1864
‡*Yours, Mine...or Ours?* #1876
‡*Baby, I'm Yours* #1893
‡‡*A Mother's Wish* #1916

Silhouette Romantic Suspense

Anything for His Children #978
Anything for Her Marriage #1006
Everything but a Husband #1050
Runaway Bridesmaid #1066
†*Plain-Jane Princess* #1096
†*Honky-Tonk Cinderella* #1120
What a Man's Gotta Do #1195
Saving Dr. Ryan #1207
**Fathers and Other Strangers* #1244
Staking His Claim #1267
**Everybody's Hero* #1328
**Swept Away* #1357
**A Husband's Watch* #1407

Silhouette Yours Truly

*Wedding Daze
*Wedding Belle
*Wedding? Impossible!

††Babies, Inc.
†How To Marry a Monarch
**The Men of Mayes County
*Weddings, Inc.
‡Guys and Daughters
‡‡Wed in the West

KAREN TEMPLETON

is a Waldenbooks bestselling author and RITA® Award nominee. As a mother of five sons, she's living proof that romance and dirty diapers are not mutually exclusive terms. An easterner transplanted to Albuquerque, New Mexico, she spends far too much time trying to coax her garden to yield roses and produce something resembling a lawn, all the while fantasizing about a weekend alone with her husband. Or at least an uninterrupted conversation.

She loves to hear from readers, who may reach her by writing c/o Silhouette Books, 233 Broadway, Suite 1001, New York, NY 10279, or online at www.karentempleton.com.

Chapter One

Eyes narrowed against the low-slung October morning sun, Winnie Porter stood in the open doorway to the Skyview Gas 'n' Grill, sipping strong coffee from a foam cup. Outside, the relentless wind scoured the barren West Texas landscape, the whiny, hollow sound like the cry of a never-satisfied newborn.

Fitting, Winnie thought, the constant hum of semis barreling along I-40 a half mile away tangling with the wind's nagging. *Come on, girl, get a move on,* it seemed to say, echoing a restlessness that had plagued her for longer than she could remember. Except now that she finally *could* get a move on...

She shifted on cowboy-booted feet, plowing one sweaty palm down a denimed thigh, the fabric soft as a baby's blanket. Over her cotton cami's neckline, the ends of her wet hair tickled her shoulders and back. Annabelle, her Border collie, nudged her thigh, panting. *We go for ride? I ride shotgun, 'kay—?*

"Here you go. And don't eat it all before you get to Amarillo."

Winnie's eyes shifted to the bulging plastic sack filled with enough food to see a family of pioneers through the winter. "Thanks," she said, steeled against the barely restrained censure flooding the nearly black eyes in front of her. Winnie took the bag, turning away as Elektra Jones blew a breath through her broad nose.

"Miss Ida ain't even been dead a week—"

"I know—"

"And all you're doin' is just setting yourself up for more hurt."

An opinion offered at least a dozen times in the last two days. "Can't hurt worse than what I've lived through the last nine years," Winnie said softly, hoisting her duffel onto her shoulder.

"But all this time, you said—"

"I was wrong," Winnie said simply. "And don't even start about needing me here, E, you know as well as I do you've been basically runnin' this place on your own anyway. Especially for the last year—"

Her voice caught as she glanced around Ida Calhoun's legacy to her only granddaughter—a run-down diner/convenience store/gas station, its proximity to the interstate its sole saving grace. Since Winnie was ten years old the place had variously been a refuge and a prison. And now it was all hers.

Even from the grave, the old girl was still getting her digs in.

"You won't even miss me," Winnie said, facing the downturned mouth underneath an inch-thick cushion of dyed blond hair.

"Now that's where you're wrong," Elektra said, eyes brimming, and Winnie thought, *Don't you dare, dammit,* giving up the fight when E muttered, "Oh, hell," and clasped Winnie to her not-insubstantial bosom.

"It's only for a week, for heaven's sake."

"Still." Elektra gave her one last squeeze, then clasped Winnie's shoulders, her hands cool and smooth on Winnie's heated skin. "You be careful, hear?" Afraid to speak, Winnie nodded.

Minutes later, with the Dixie Chicks holding forth from the old pickup's radio and Annabelle grinning into the wind from her passenger side perch, Winnie glided onto the interstate behind a big rig with Alabama plates, headed west on what even she knew was likely to be a fool's errand.

Hours later, she climbed out of the truck in front of a mud-colored gnome of an adobe squatting in the woods, wearing an incongruous, steeply pitched, tin-roof hat. With a woof of anticipation, Annabelle streaked into the dense, bushy piñons and yellowing live oaks, their leaves rustling in the cleanest breeze Winnie had ever smelled; she squinted into the glare of luminescent blue overhead, nearly the same color as the peeling paint on the house's front door. *This, I can deal with,* she thought, smiling, as the sharply cool air—a good twenty degrees cooler here than home—goosed her bare arms and back.

Winnie backtracked to tug a long-sleeved shirt off the front seat, as a white Toyota Highlander crunched up behind her. The real estate agent, she guessed, her thought was confirmed a moment later when a very pregnant, very pretty, dark-haired gal carefully extricated herself from behind the wheel and shouted over, "You must be Winnie! I'm Tess Montoya, we spoke over the phone." She opened her back door to spring an equally dark-haired preschooler from the backseat, then laughed. "I warned you not to expect much!"

"Are you kidding?" Winnie shrugged into her shirt, smiling for the adorable little boy, shyly clinging to his mother's long skirt. Then she turned to take in the swarms of deep-pink cosmos nodding atop feathery stems on either side of the door, the pair of small windows—also blue-framed, also peeling—hunkered inside foot-thick walls, like the eyes of a fat-cheeked baby—

"I love it already!" she said with another grin in Tess's direction as she grabbed duffel and sleeping bag from behind the seat, then followed the chattering agent inside.

"Unfortunately, both the electricity and plumbing can be temperamental," Tess was saying, palming her stomach. Winnie looked away. "But my aunt—she's the owner's housekeeper—stayed here for a while before she moved in with the family. So I knew it would be livable. At least for a week! Although it's still beyond me why you wanted to stay in Tierra Rosa. Now if you'd said Taos or Santa Fe—"

"This is fine. Really," Winnie said, her gear thunking to the bare wooden floor, gouged and unpolished, as she let her eyes adjust to the milky light inside. In an instant she catalogued the stark, white, unadorned plaster walls and kiva fireplace, the mission-style sofa and matching chair with scuffed leather seats, the oversize rocker, the log-headboarded double bed. The "kitchen" consisted of an old pie cupboard between an iron-stained sink and an ancient gas stove, a battle-weary whitewashed table with two mismatched chairs. A low-framed door, she discovered, led to a bug-size bathroom, clearly an afterthought, with one of those old-time claw-footed tubs.

But the place was spotless, with fluffy towels hanging from black iron rings, a brand-new cake of Dove on the sink. And the thick comforter and fluffy pillows on the bed practically begged her to come try it out.

"It's…cozy," she said, and Tess laughed.

"Nice word for it. Listen, sorry I have to scoot, but I've got a million things to do before this little squirt pops out. But there's my card," she said, laying a business card on the table, then trundling toward the open front door, through which floated childish laughter. "Call me if you need anything. Or my aunt, she's just up the hill, I left you her number, too— Oh! Miguel! No, baby, leave the doggie alone!"

"I think it's the other way around," Winnie said, laughing, as she called Annabelle off the giggling—and now dog-spit-slimed—little boy.

"I keep thinking about getting him a dog, but with his father away and a new baby…" Tess sighed. "Anyway… enjoy your stay!"

Winnie watched the SUV rumble down the dirt road, then went back inside. Annabelle promptly hopped up on the bed, turned three times in place and flopped down, grinning, eager-eyed. *We live here now?*

"Only for a week," Winnie said over the pinch of anxiety in her stomach, Elektra's warning ringing in her ears. "Maybe."

She tugged open the back door and walked out into the small clearing carved out of the forest, where the sweet, clean breeze caught her loose hair the way a mother might sift a child's through her fingers. A shrill bird call made her glance up in time to catch a flutter of blue wings. A jay, maybe, rustling in the branches, searching for pine nuts. She shut her eyes, savoring, telling herself even if her reason for being here didn't pan out, that after the past year—years—there were worse things than spending a week in heaven.

Winnie's smile faded, however, when she opened her eyes and noticed the fresh bicycle tracks in the soft dirt, leading to a path that disappeared into the trees. She turned, frowning, her gaze following the tracks, which stopped just short of the house, next to a woodpile probably loaded with eight-legged things. Or, far worse, *no*-legged things. With scales and forked tongues.

In the woods behind, something cracked. Winnie wheeled, her back prickling, her great fear of slithery wildlife momentarily forgotten as Annabelle joyfully vanished into the undergrowth in hot pursuit…only to flinch at the barrage of pine nuts from overhead, courtesy of a huge, and very pissed-off, squirrel. The dog glanced up, confused, then hauled ass back to the house to cower behind Winnie's legs.

The sky embraced her laughter.

His breath coming in short, angry pants, the child tightly gripped the handlebars of his birthday bike—a real mountain bike, just like he'd wanted—as he watched the lady and her dog through the trees. He let go long enough to swipe a hand across his nose, a hot burst exploding inside his chest. *You get away from my house!* he wanted to yell, except his throat was all frozen up—

"Robbie! Rob-*bie!*"

Robson jerked his head toward Florita's call, her voice pretty faint this far from the house. If he didn't get back soon, she'd get worried, and then she'd tell his dad, and *he'd* get worried, and that would suck. So after one last glance at the lady laughing at her dumb dog, he turned around, pumping the pedals as fast as he could to get back.

To get away.

The chickens scattered, clucking their heads off, when he streaked through the yard, dumping his bike and running around to the back. "An' where were you?" Florita asked when he came into the sunny kitchen, the pretty blue-and-yellow tiles making Robson feel better and sad at the same time, because Mom had picked them out.

"Just out ridin'," Robson said, panting, going to the big silvery fridge for a bottle of juice. He could feel Florita's dark eyes on his back, like she could see right through him. He really liked Flo, but she saw too much, sometimes. And nice as she was, she wasn't Mom. Mom had been all soft and real-looking, her long, black-and-silver hair slippery-smooth when Robson touched it. Flo's hair was dark, too, but it was all stiff and pokey. She wore way too much makeup, too, and clothes like all the teenage girls did at the mall, like she was scared of getting old, or something.

Mom had always said getting old didn't scare her at all, it was just part of life. Robson swallowed past the lump in his throat, only then he realized Flo had been saying something.

"Huh?"

Flo rolled her eyes. "One of these days, you're gonna clean out your ears an' hear what I say the firs' time, an' I'm gonna fall right over from the shock." Since Flo said stuff like that all the time, he knew she wasn't really mad. "I *said,* your father's goin' down to Garcia's, you wanna go with him?"

"No, that's okay," Robbie said, and Flo gave him one of her looks, the one that said she understood. That ever since Mom died, Dad spent more and more time up in his studio, painting, and not so much time with Robson. Not like he used to, anyway. Flo said Dad was just trying to "work though" his feelings about Mom dying and stuff. Which made Robson mad, a little, because you know what? He missed Mom, too. A lot. And it hurt that he didn't feel like he could talk to Dad about it. But whenever he tried, Dad would get all mopey-dopey, and that only made everything worse. So finally Robson stopped trying. Because what was the point?

"You can't stop trying," Flo said softly, like she'd read his mind, which kinda freaked Robbie out. He also knew she'd only nag him if he didn't go, so he finished his juice, went and peed, then dragged himself out to Dad's studio, pushing himself from one side of the passage to the other as he went, even though Flo would get on his case about the handprints.

Once there, he had to blink until his eyes got used to the bright light—with all the windows along the top, it was almost like being outside. Especially since the room was so tall. Robbie liked how it smelled in here, like oil paint and wood and that stuff Dad used to make the canvases white before he painted on them. Rock music playing from a CD player on the floor practically bounced off the walls and ceiling, it was so loud, tickling Robbie's feet and moving right on up through his body. When he was littler, he used to like yelling out his name in here, just to hear it echo.

Paint all over his jeans and long-sleeved T-shirt, Dad was cleaning up one of his big paintbrushes, frowning a little at the painting he was working on. At least, Robbie thought he was frowning—it was hard to tell with Dad's dark, curly hair hanging in his face. Robbie fingered his own much lighter-colored hair, which was almost as long. Flo was constantly fussing at both of them to get it cut, but Dad said this was their mountain-man look. He didn't shave every day, either. Flo had a lot to say about that, too.

Robbie looked at the painting. Some of Dad's canvases were so humongous he had to build this thing called a scaffolding to reach the top. But this one was small enough to sit on one of Dad's special-made easels. The colors were real bright, oranges and purples and pinks and greens, kinda like the view from his window when the sun was going down. But instead of being pretty, the colors looked like they were fighting each other.

"D'you like it?" Dad asked. His father sounded different from everybody else around here because he was from Ireland. It was neat, watching his friends' eyes get all big the first time they'd hear Dad say something.

He twisted to see Dad watching him with that sad look in his eyes Robbie hated, so he turned his head back around, fast, like when you touch something hot and drop it right away, before it can burn you.

"Who's it for?"

"Just for me," Dad said.

And Robbie said, "Oh." Then he added, "Flo said you're goin' down to Garcia's?"

"Yeah, they got in a shipment for me today." Dad often had art supplies and stuff sent to the old store down on the highway, rather than to the house, partly because it was sometimes hard for the delivery trucks to get up here, partly so people wouldn't be able to find him. Dad didn't like people poking around in his business, he said. "Want to come along?"

"Sure," he said, like it was no big deal. Except when he looked at Dad, he was smiling, sort of. At least enough to make creases in his fuzzy cheeks. But his eyes still looked like they were saying he was sorry. Like Mom's dying had somehow been Dad's fault. Robbie wanted to tell Dad to stop being dumb. Instead, he asked, "Can I get a Nutty Buddy?"

"You're on," Dad said back, reaching down to swing Robbie up into his arms, like he used to do, and Robbie hugged his neck as tight as he could, not even caring that Dad's face was all prickly, like a porcupine.

The sign in the window was hand-lettered and to the point:

Dogs and Kids Allowed Only With an Adult

Gotta love a town that's got its priorities straight, Winnie thought as she freed Annabelle from the truck in front of the long, stuccoed building with a columned front porch, all by its lonesome out on the highway. And according to the larger—but still hand-lettered—sign stuck in the dirt bordering the road, Tierra Rosa's only gas station. She'd keep that in mind.

On one side of the porch sat a series of wooden rocking chairs, flanked by wooden crates of corn, melons and apples; on two of the chairs sat a pair of toothless, leathery-faced old men, rocking off-sync and scrutinizing Winnie from underneath battered cowboy hats as she and Annabelle walked up the steps. She nodded; they nodded back.

Inside, the plank-floored building was the modern equivalent of the old-fashioned general store. A quick perusal revealed everything from diapers to fishing tackle, Hungry-Man dinners to motor oil, Levis to Rice Krispies. In addition to food, gas and pretty much everything else, a sign at the front counter also proclaimed the place's official U.S. Post Office status, P.O. Boxes Available.

Aside from the old dudes outside, Winnie and Annabelle were the only customers; by the cash register, a very cute, overly cleavaged, brunette teenager in a low-cut top and open hoodie leaned on the counter, her chin digging into her palm as she flipped through what looked like a textbook, frantically taking notes in a spiral notebook beside it. Something told Winnie that whatever the gal's assignment was, she wasn't finding the tall, buff, teenage boy with a shaved head trying to get cozier all that much of a distraction.

"Quit it, Jesse!" she said, making a great show of moving out of range. "I've got this *major* test tomorrow—!"

"Aw, c'mon, Rach…just one little kiss? Please?"

Then she giggled, which the boy took as leave to swoop in for that kiss.

Winnie smartly wheeled her hundred-year-old grocery buggy toward the back, thinking, *Ain't love grand?* over a wave of déjà vu so strong she was half inclined to stomp back to the register and smack some sense into one or both of the kids. Because nobody knew more than her where swooping and such led to.

Then she sighed and went about her business, reminding herself that not every teenage girl who indulges in a little kissy-face gets knocked up. That some were smart enough not to let things go that far. Or at least to make sure there were no consequences if they did.

"You need any help finding stuff?" the girl called out, almost like she cared. Winnie poked her head up over a shelf brimming with Old El Paso products.

"Um...dog food?"

"Back wall, to your right. Ice cream's on special this week, too. Two half gallons for six bucks."

"Thanks," Winnie said, hauling a twenty-pound bag of Purina into her cart, then nudging it toward the frozen-food case, since the gal had taken such pains to steer her in that direction. Lost in a quandary between mint chocolate chip and Snickers, she barely heard the bell jingle over the door. So it took a second for the deep, Irish-accented male voice asking about a package to register.

"Oh, yeah, Mr. Black," the girl said. "It's right here, let me get it for you...."

After a white-hot jolt of adrenaline, Winnie ducked slightly behind a display of fishing rods to peer toward the front, too late realizing that Annabelle had sauntered back up to see if anybody needed herding, kisses, whatever. A moment later a young kid with shaggy, pale-blond hair popped into view, yanking open the case to grab one of the loose Nutty Buddies inside. At Winnie's sucked-in breath, the kid's head whipped around, eyes wide, and something inside her exploded.

Five minutes on the Internet, and there'd been the magazine article, complete with a photo of the reclusive Western landscape painter and his wife, a textile artist/social activist, her broad smile much more relaxed and friendly than her significantly younger husband's. And scattered throughout the article, shots of the marvel of wood and glass—one whole side devoted to the high-ceilinged studio built especially to accommodate the "Irish Cowboy's" massive canvases—that Aidan and June Black had built in the mountains bordering the picturesque northern New Mexican village of Tierra Rosa.

Then Winnie's heart had stopped at the single profile image of the Blacks' only child, a son. Adopted, although the article hadn't mentioned that. Seven at the time of the shoot two years earlier, his hair had been almost angel-white in the sunlight.

The same color Winnie's had been at that age—

"Yarp!"

Annabelle had reappeared to bow in front of the boy, tail wagging. *Boy play with me? Please?* Frowning, his thin shoulders weighted in some way she couldn't exactly define, the kid looked from the dog to her, then back at the dog, quivering in anticipation.

"It's okay," Winnie said, not sure how she was breathing. "She wouldn't hurt a bug if she stepped on it."

Slowly, the boy got down on one knee to pat Annabelle's head, and the dog became a blur—*Boy likes me! Boy really, really likes me!*—trying to lick everywhere at once. But he'd barely started giggling before he scrambled back upright, as though realizing he wasn't supposed to be ca-vorting with strange dogs. Or a stranger's dog, at least. Now the eyes focused on Winnie's were accusatory, sus-picious. Pained. And nearly the same weird blue-gray as hers, except for the flecks of gold near the iris.

"You the lady stayin' in the Old House?"

The *Old* House. Like it was a name, not a description.

"Just for a little while." *He has my nose, too. For trouble, I bet.* "You…saw me?"

"Yeah. Earlier." The pointed chin came up. "Through the trees. I was on my bike."

Bicycle tracks. Check.

"Oh. Do you, um, like to play around there?"

"Sometimes," he said with a shrug. *Not that I care.*

Winnie's mouth curved, at his beauty, his bravado. At how silly his long hair looked, nearly to his shoulders, as shiny and wavy as a girl's. But every inch a boy, all the same, in his skater-dude outfit, the holes in his jeans' knees. Still, she imagined the only thing keeping him from getting the crap beat out of him at school was his height, which made him look more like ten, maybe even eleven, than just-turned-nine.

Her face burning, Winnie turned back to the freezer case, grabbing—of all things—a carton of strawberry cheesecake ice cream, swallowing back the reassurance that wanted so bad to pop out of her mouth, that he could still come down and play, anytime—

"Robbie? Where'd you go—?"

They both looked up as Aidan Black—far shaggier and craggier than she remembered—materialized at the end of the aisle, nearly sending Winnie's heart catapulting from her sternum. A second's glance told her this was definitely not the mellow, grinning young man, his musical accent as smooth as one of Elektra's chocolate shakes, she'd met barely two weeks before delivering the baby who'd become his son. The warm, laughing green eyes now dull and shuttered, this, she thought, was the very devil himself.

A devil who, despite how much she'd changed, too, instantly recognized her.

And wasn't the least bit happy about it.

Her hair wasn't punked up and jet-black as it had been then, but there was no mistaking those dusty-blue eyes, the set to her jaw, the way her long arms and legs seemed barely joined to her long-waisted torso, like a marionette.

A curse exploded underneath Aidan's skull, just as Robbie said, "She's the lady livin' in the Old House," and Aidan thought, *Flo is a dead woman.*

"We need to go," he muttered, grabbing his son—*his* son—by the hand and practically hauling the lad up front to pay for his ice cream, hoping to hell "the lady" got the message that if she so much as opened her mouth—

He threw a couple of ones at Johnny Griego's daughter at the register and kept going, swinging Robbie up into the truck's cab and storming around to his side.

"Dad?" Robbie said, cautiously, once they were back on the highway. "What's wrong?"

Where would you like me to start? Aidan thought. "Nothing, laddie," he muttered, bracing himself as they passed a pasture where a half dozen or so horses aimlessly grazed...but not a peep from the other side of the truck. Then they crested a hill, on the other side of which lay a field chock-full of pumpkins. He glanced over, trying to decide if Robbie's gaze was as fixed on those pumpkins as it appeared.

"We could stop, if you like," he said carefully. When Robbie stayed quiet, Aidan added, "Shop early for the best selection?"

A second or two passed before Robbie shook his head. Aidan didn't have to look at the lad to see the tears in his eyes.

His own stinging, as well, they kept driving, a heaping great sadness clawing at Aidan's insides.

Aidan waited until he heard the distant boops and beeps of Robbie's video game before confronting his house-keeper. "And it didn't occur t'ya to tell me *who* Tess had let the Old House to?"

As it was, Aidan had only begrudgingly ceded to Flo's entreaties, via her niece, to rent out the house to some woman from Texas determined to stay in Tierra Rosa and *only* Tierra Rosa. A normal man might have been at least curious about that. But Aidan was not a normal man, rarely concerning himself with the goings-on of the town he'd called home for more than a decade. So why would he have been even remotely interested in some woman keen on finding lodgings right here in town, and no where else?

Because I'm an eejit, he thought, as Florita slammed

shut the oven door on their taco casserole, then turned, fully armed for the counterattack.

"An' how were we supposed to know she was Robson's birth mother? Even if Tessie had told me her name, it would have meant bupkis to me, since nobody ever told me what it was. Right? So you can stop with the guilt trip, boss."

Aidan dropped heavily onto a kitchen chair, grinding the heel of one turpentine-scented hand into the space between his brows. True, since Flo hadn't come to work for them until after Winnie Porter had removed herself from the equation, there'd been no reason to tell her who Robbie's birth mother was.

But an anxious-eyed Flo had already sat across from him, their squabble forgotten. "You scared this woman's gonna pull a fas' one on you?"

"Not scared. Angry. That she showed up out of the blue. That she'd…" His hand fisted in front of him. "She'd no right to do this."

"But if it was an open adoption—?"

"One she herself opted out of more than eight years ago."

Flo seemed to consider this for a moment, then said, "You think she knows about Miss June? That she's showin' up now because Robbie's mama's dead?"

"I've no idea," Aidan said on an expelled breath, then surged to his feet, grabbing his wool jacket from the hook. "Y'mind holding dinner for a bit?"

"Where you goin'?"

But Aidan was already out the door, the blood chugging through his veins faster than it had in more than a year.

Chapter Two

It'd been years since Aidan had even been down to the eighty-year-old, single-room adobe where he and June had lived when they first moved to Tierra Rosa. They'd bought the property for its own sake, holing up in the Old House until Aidan's career had taken off well enough to build the New House, a half mile farther up the mountain. A half mile farther away from civilization. Not that either Aidan or June had been hideously famous, not then, not ever. Certainly not like the A-list actresses and shock jocks and such who called New Mexico home—they simply valued their privacy. Aidan, especially. In fact, he'd balked about that damn magazine spread, but June…

The back of his throat clogged as, despite top-of-the-line shocks, the truck shimmied and jolted down the dirt road, partially obscured by clumps of live oak and lemon-flowered chamisa, until shuddering to a stop in front of the house.

Snoozing in a coppery patch of sun on the low porch,

the Border collie instantly jumped to attention, yapping; a second later, the screen door banged open and Winnie Porter appeared, hands shoved in her jeans' pockets, the ebbing sunlight glancing off features a lot harder-edged than he remembered. But then, when he'd last seen her she'd been a very pregnant eighteen-year-old, her defiance worn down—according to June—by water weight and too many sleepless nights.

As he'd been then, Aidan was struck by her height, her almost mannish stance in cowboy boots that were all about utility rather than style, how there was nothing soft about her, anywhere. Even her hair was stick-straight, a million strands of wheat blowing helter-skelter around heavy-lidded eyes and pronounced cheekbones.

"Figured you'd be here soon enough."

Her gaze was dead-on, unflinching. Certainly not a look designed to provoke concern about a woman being out here all alone, never mind that the only place safer would be a padded cell.

Aidan climbed down from his truck, coming just close enough for purposes of communication. Close enough to catch the determined set to her mouth. The instant that mouth opened, though, he cut her off with, "How the bloody *hell* did you find us?"

She shoved a stray chunk of her hair behind her ear. Unlike before, when black gunk had rimmed her eyes and she'd sported more studs than a country singer's costume, she wore no jewelry, no makeup that Aidan could tell.

"Online," she said, and his brain snapped back to attention. "That magazine article from a couple years back? At least, that you were living in Tierra Rosa—"

"You gave up the right to be part of Robson's life more than eight years ago, when you begged—*begged*—us not to send you any more information about him."

He saw the flash of regret. "I know. But if you'd give me a chance—"

"To do what? To disrupt a nine-year-old's life?"

"*No!*" The word boomed between them. "That was never my intention! It still isn't," she said, but Aidan saw something in those dusky eyes that said there was more, the kind of *more* that was tensing his whole body. "Yeah, I knew it was a long shot, showing up out of the blue—"

"Long shot, hell. Try idiotic."

Winnie backhanded her bangs out of her eyes. "And if there'd been any way of contacting you, I would've cleared things with you and June first—"

"Robbie's *mother* is dead."

She literally reeled. "Oh, God…I had no idea—"

"Just as you had no idea this house was on my property, I suppose."

"I didn't," she said, her brows nearly meeting underneath the tangle of hair on her forehead. "Oh, for heaven's sake—it wasn't like I was gonna tell anybody I was looking for you! Not until I got here, at least. So how *would* I have known?"

Aidan shifted to cross his arms. Her damn dog sidled up to him, wagging its tail, trying to play mediator. "So you just came here on the off chance that…what?"

She rammed her hands into her back pockets, somehow managing to look sheepish and determined at the same time. "That somehow I'd be able to see him. That's all. Just…see him."

"D'you think I'm daft?"

She almost smiled. "I doubt anybody'd call *your* sanity into question." The dog trotted back, all eyes for her mistress; Winnie bent over to pet her, her features softening in the peachy light. Then she lifted her eyes again, her voice gentle as rainwater when she said, "June hasn't been gone very long, I take it?"

Aidan braced himself against the wave of pain, even

though it no longer hit as high or hard as it once did. The guilt that it didn't, though, sometimes felt worse.

"A year ago July. She was already sick when the magazine people came around." He paused, his eyes riveted to hers. "It's been a rough couple of years. Especially on the boy."

Winnie broke the stare first, her gaze shifting toward the fiery glow behind the trees. "I can imagine," she murmured, before her gaze met his again. "My grandmother died, too. A week or so ago."

An event, he instantly surmised, that had something to do with Winnie's sudden appearance. An image popped into Aidan's head of the tall, commandeering woman with hair the color of a rooster's comb and a gaze hot enough to peel flesh from bone. "My condolences."

Winnie's mouth stretched tight. "Not necessary. As you may have gathered, Miss Ida was definitely a 'my way or the highway' kind of gal. And 'her way' did not include helping raise her teenage granddaughter's bastard."

Aidan tensed. "You swore the adoption was your idea."

"I was eighteen. Legal, maybe, but nowhere near ready to raise a kid on my own. And on my own is exactly what it would've been, since the baby's father had vanished faster than a summer thunderstorm and my grandmother would have kicked me and the baby out on our butts."

"You really think she would gone that far?"

Winnie blew a humorless laugh through her nose. "You met her. What do you think? And at the time," she said, in that careful voice people use when the emotions are far too close to the surface, "I was totally on board with the open-adoption idea. Bein' able to keep tabs on my baby, hear from time to time how he was getting on…" She stopped, once more shoving her breeze-stirred hair out of her face, and Aidan braced himself, thinking, *No. Don't.* Except he wasn't at all sure whether the order was meant for Winnie or himself.

"So what happened?"

"I made the mistake of holding my baby, that's what. Knowing what's best and what you feel…" Her eyes glistened. "But I thought, for my son's sake, *I can do this, I can let him go.* Except it's a little hard to let go when there's this thread keeping you tied to each other. After a few months I knew if I didn't cut that thread completely, I'd go crazy."

"Then why are you here now?"

"Because when Ida died," she shot back, "it hit me that I had nobody else in the entire world I could call family. No aunts or uncles, no cousins, nothing. And maybe this doesn't make sense to anybody but me, but I just…I just wanted to make sure my kid was okay, that's all. For my own peace of mind."

"Fine," Aidan said in a low voice. "You've seen him. So you can go back home with a clean conscience."

Winnie's head tilted on her long neck, the serrated ends of her hair sliding across her shoulders. "You would think," she said sadly, and realization slammed into Aidan that it wasn't *anger* making his skin crawl.

It was fear.

Even in the waning light, there was no mistaking Aidan Black's don't-mess-with-my-cub expression. If nothing else, at least Winnie could comfort herself knowing the adoption had taken so strong. Hey, if the roles had been reversed, she'd probably see her as a threat, too.

Except the roles weren't reversed, they were what they were, and the fact was, a glimpse hadn't been enough. Why she'd ever thought it would be, she'd have to dissect at some future date. Not that she wasn't aware how thin the ice was she was skating on, just being here to begin with. But now that she *was* here—

"I don't suppose you'd consider letting me spend some time with Robbie?"

"You're not serious?"

Winnie felt as if she was trying to swallow five-year-old peanut butter. "Just as a friend. As *your* son, not mine. And you have every right to tell me to go to hell—"

"Back to Texas would be sufficient, I think."

Tears threatened. *No,* she thought. "I know you don't trust me—"

"And you're wastin' both of our times," Aidan said, hands up, starting toward his truck.

"You *could* try to get to know me!" she shouted toward his back. "The me I am now, not the whacked-out teenager you met exactly once, and only for an hour at that. I swear," she called out when he reached the driver-side door, "I would never do anything to hurt my own child! To hurt *any* child!"

Aidan turned. "Maybe not intentionally. But the effect would be the same."

"How?" she said, coming off the porch, hearing *Fool, fool, fool* echo inside her head, helpless as usual to stop her mouth once it got going. "Aidan, I promise I'm no more interested in turning back the clock than you are. I'll even respect if you've never told him he's adopted--"

"Of *course* he knows he's adopted!" Aidan said, long fingers squeezing the door handle. "But not only has he shown absolutely no curiosity about his birth parents, he's still torn up about his mother's death. Don'cha think that's enough stress for a nine-year-old to deal with at one time?"

"Yes, I do. I've been there. So I've got a pretty good idea how Robson's probably feeling." She paused, suddenly identifying the nameless emotion she'd seen in the boy's eyes back at the store. "Hell, he drags his pain around with him like a ball and chain. And yeah, it's that obvious," she said at Aidan's raised brows, deciding it probably wouldn't do to point out that Aidan did, too. She swallowed. Came close. "If you don't want him to know I'm his birth mother right now, I'm fine with that."

For the first time, she sensed Aidan's wavering.

"Please," she said softly, briefly touching his arm, muscles stiff underneath a layer of weathered denim. "I know I'm asking a lot, and you've got every right to say no—"

"That I do," he said, his eyes going flinty again. "I'm sorry, Winnie," he said, like he wasn't sorry at all. "I can't take the chance."

It was stupid, how much it hurt, especially considering how low she'd thought her expectations had been. And anyway, even if she did get to see Robson, what if this new objective turned out to be no more satisfying than the first? What if she ended up returning to Texas with a heart even more broken than before, just like Elektra'd said?

Except then she realized it was too late, she'd already opened that particular can of worms and there was no cramming them back inside.

Nodding, her gaze sliding away, she backed up, her arms crossed. "Does he even know my name?"

"No."

Her eyes lifted again. "You ever gonna tell him about me?"

"Only if he asks."

After a moment, Winnie nodded again, hoping to make it back inside before the tears fell.

"So you'll be leaving in the morning?" she heard behind her.

"I suppose. Now if you'll excuse me, it's been a long day—"

"Watch out for the electricity, it's a bit dodgy."

Winnie turned, thoroughly confused. "Uh, yeah…Tess already told me—"

"And I assume you have a cell phone?"

"Charging even as we speak—"

"Give me your number, then," Aidan said, digging his own phone out of his pocket.

"Why?"

"You're on my property, I'm responsible for your welfare. So just give me your number, damn it."

Shaking her head, Winnie stomped inside, fished a pen out of her purse and scribbled her number on a Burger King napkin from a pit stop in Moriarty, then went back outside and handed it to him.

"Then you better give me yours, too. Just in case a herd of rabid raccoons storms the house during the night."

She thought maybe his mouth twitched. "505-555-2076."

She scribbled it on a second napkin, although since she had a mind like flypaper she'd already memorized it. After that they stared each other down for another couple of seconds until Aidan finally opened his door and climbed into his truck.

"Hey," she called over before he could shut his door.

"What?"

"I may have made some really, really dumb choices in my life, but something tells me choosing you and June as my baby's parents wasn't one of them."

Then she went inside, thinking, *Chew on that, buster.*

Some time later, sitting on the bed in a pair of seen-better-days sweats, the tub of cheesecake ice cream rapidly vanishing as she stared at the flames belly-dancing in the fireplace, Winnie realized she'd stalled out at *O-kay...now what?*

By rights, she supposed she should at least be a little spooked, out here in the middle of nowhere all by her lonesome, with nothing but a lazy dog—she cast an affectionate glance at Annabelle, smushed up against her thighs—to protect her. But Winnie had never been the spookable sort. Not by things like slasher movies or ghost stories or things that went bump in the night, anyway.

Nor was she generally prone to boredom, since having lived most of her life in her own branch of nowhere she'd learned early on how to keep herself occupied. There'd always been people to see, fat to chew, businesses to keep tabs on, ailing grandmothers to tend to…even if by the end of Ida's illness Winnie's biggest fantasy centered on not having one blessed thing to do.

Well, honeybunch, she thought, setting the melting ice cream on the nightstand and curling forward to hug her knees, *wish granted.* Because here she was, with nothing and nobody to tend to.

Except her own thoughts.

Like about how being absolutely alone like this made her realize just how absolutely alone she was.

Now *that* was spooky.

Not that her family life had been any *Waltons* episode, although you'd think the way Ida'd watched those damn DVDs over and over, something would've rubbed off on her. But apparently they had rubbed off on Winnie, who still believed, deep in her heart, that families like that existed, somewhere. Families where all those binding ties held you up. Not tripped you up.

And coming here, seeing Robson…

The funny thing was, she thought, blowing her nose into another napkin, it wasn't like she'd laid eyes on Robbie and immediately fallen in love with him. Oh, she'd felt a definite pang of something, she just hadn't defined it yet. Curiosity, maybe. Combined with a little shock. But mostly she'd thought, *Wow. That's my kid.*

And speaking of pangs…was it just her, or was Aidan seeing her appearance as much of a threat to *him* as to his son? Why she should think this, she had no idea, but all told she supposed it was just as well she was leaving. A body could only take so much weirdness at one time—

"Oh, Lord!" she yelped at the sudden knock on the door.

She glanced at the dog, who yawned and snuggled more deeply into the soft, welcoming mounds of comforter, rolling one eye in Winnie's direction. *I stay here, keep the bed warm for you, 'kay?*

"Sure thing, wouldn't want to disturb you," Winnie muttered, before, on a profound sigh, she crawled out from underneath the nice warm covers to creep across the bare floor in sock-clad tootsies.

"Who is it?" she yelled through the—thankfully—solid front door.

"Florita Pena," came a warm, richly accented voice. "Mr. Aidan's housekeeper? I'm…jus' checking to see if you have enough towels and…things?"

Hmm. The woman *sounded* harmless enough. Then again, some people might've thought her grandmother was harmless, too. If they were deluded or drunk enough. Steeling herself, she opened the door to a middle-aged woman in tight everything, like a drag queen doing a bad Rita Moreno impersonation.

Winnie was guessing the whole linens thing was just a ruse.

"Does your boss know you're here?" she asked the housekeeper.

Wide, very red lips spread across a heavily moisturized face. "Do I look like I jus' fell off the truck?"

"I'll make tea," Winnie said, holding open the door, taking care to keep her tootsies well out of range of the four-inch stilettos.

"And where the hell have you been?" Aidan hurled at his housekeeper when she "sneaked" back in through the kitchen door. "As if I couldn't guess."

Shucking off her gold leather jacket and hanging it on the hook by the door, Florita slid her eyes to his. She'd pounced on him like a cat on a lizard the moment he'd returned from his earlier visit to Winnie, although he hadn't been able to fill her in properly until after supper, when Robson had gone up to his room to do homework. She'd listened, said little—which should have set off alarms—then vanished the minute Aidan's back was turned. Now she shrugged. "My name's not Cinderella, big shot, I don' have to explain my comings an' goings to you. I jus' decided to check this chick out for myself."

Then, because she was Flo, she grabbed a sponge and started to wipe down already sanitized counters. "And?" Aidan said with exaggerated patience.

"She's got *cojones,*" she said at last, bony shoulders bumping. "It took guts, her coming here like this."

"And…?" he said again.

Crimson lips pursed. "I think she knows nothing's gonna change, no matter what. But I also think she felt she had to do this, you know? Like she heard a voice, maybe."

The Irish with their superstitions have nothing on the Latinos, Aidan thought, muttering, "Doesn't mean we're hearing the same voices." When Flo didn't reply, he said, "Jaysus, Flo, the woman's already changed her mind twice about what she wants, once when Robson was still a baby, the second time barely two hours ago. Winnie Porter's as unstable as a three-legged table. If not downright crazy, coming here without even knowing if we were around or not."

"Just because she did something crazy doesn't mean she *is* crazy," Flo said, but she didn't look any too sure of that.

"Surely y'don't think I should let her see him?"

"I don't know, boss. An' anyway, it's not up to me."

Aidan released a breath. "Winnie swore up one side and down t'other she wouldn't tell Robbie who she was, but what's to prevent her from having another change of heart? All it takes is one slip, and the damage is done."

Rinsing out her sponge at the stainless steel sink, Flo tossed him a wordless glance over her shoulder.

"He never even *asks* about his birth mother, Flo—"

"An' you don' exactly encourage him, do you?"

"Why would I do that when everything's fine the way it is?"

Slamming the sponge down by the faucet, the housekeeper spun around, grabbing a dish towel to dry her hands. *"Fine?"* She barked out a laugh. "After a year, Robbie still mopes aroun', keeping to himself…that sure don' sound like *fine* to me. *Dios mío*—when was the las' time there was any real laughter in this house? I'll tell you when," she said, tears pooling in her dark eyes. "Not since Miss June was alive. If you call that *fine,* I call you *loco.*"

Aidan's mouth pulled tight. True, Robson and he rarely talked anymore. Even tonight, Aidan's awkward attempts to draw his son into some sort of conversation had been a bust, like always, his offer to help the lad with his homework rejected out of hand. No, things were far from fine. But…

"She had her chance, Flo. We were more than willing to keep her in the loop, and she backed out of the deal. And whose side are you on, anyway?"

Flo crossed her arms over a bosom so flat it was nearly concave. "Robbie's my baby, too, I don' want to see him hurt any more than you do. An' I'm not saying I totally trust this girl—"

"You think she'd try to make contact behind my back?" Aidan said over the jolt to his heart.

"At this point," Flo said, frowning, "no. I don' think so. She knows forcing the issue's not gonna get her what she wants. No, it's Robbie I'm worried about."

"Robbie?"

"When you get back from Garcia's, he comes in here, starts asking me if I knew there was some lady staying in the Old House, how come nobody ever stayed there before now." When she paused, Aidan caught the ambivalence in her eyes, that she was just as conflicted as he was. "If I knew who she was. I tell him no, but I can see the wheels turning," she said, pointing to her head, then crossing her arms. "An' once those wheels get started…" Her sentence ended in a shrug. "You know what they say—*el gato satisfecho no le preocupa ratón.*"

Aidan was by no means fluent in Spanish, but after ten years of living in a town where the population was seventy-five percent Hispanic, even he got that one: *The satisfied cat ignores the mouse.*

"Except Winnie's leaving in the morning," Aidan said, "so the point's moot."

"You think if she disappears, so will his questions?" When Aidan grimaced a second time, Flo added, "Maybe you should ask yourself…what would Miss June do? What would she wan' *you* to do?"

A few minutes later, tall boy in hand, Aidan stood outside on the second story deck looking down toward the Old House, slivers of window light barely visible through the trees. And in that house, a woman with the courage to ask for something even she'd acknowledged she had no right to ask. As much as her plea had annoyed him, it had also threatened some part of himself he'd thought he'd secured good and tight months ago.

One hip propped against the railing, Aidan took a swig of his beer, replaying that whole cat-and-mouse thing in his head. Except people weren't cats. In fact, that was the trouble with humans—the more they knew, the more they wanted to know. Winnie Porter had already demonstrated that, hadn't she?

Aidan pushed out a groan into the rapidly cooling air. Winnie's coming here was definitely an aggravation he did not need. However…what *would* June do? Where would her sympathies lie?

Stupid question, he thought on an airless laugh. As thrilled as his wife had been about adopting Robson, hadn't she been the one to worry about how Winnie was dealing with it, if she had anybody to talk to who understood what she was going through? Then when Winnie cut off communication, he'd thought surely Winnie herself couldn't be taking it any harder than June.

His mouth curved. In so many ways, June had been as tough as they came, taking on causes nobody else would touch, having no qualms about stirring up trouble if she thought stirring was warranted. But her heart was soft as cotton. She was more than a loving person, it was as though love was her purpose in life. Not the kind of love blind to human failings, but the kind that sees through those failings to the core of a person. His wife had no patience with stupidity, but deep down she believed in the basic goodness of mankind.

Aidan's lungs filled with the sweetly acrid air, that pungent blend of moldering leaves and fireplace smoke that would always remind him of his wife. For her, not spring, but autumn had always been about new beginnings. She saw in the blaze of color that swept the mountains not death, but beauty. Comfort. Joy.

And right now, he felt her presence so strongly he could barely breathe.

June had never specifically spelled out her wishes regarding Robbie and his birth mother, but if she were here…

But she's not, Aidan thought bitterly. And the situation was very different than if she had been. His first duty was to protect Robbie, at all costs. He didn't owe Winnie Porter a damn thing.

Oh, for godsake, babe, the breeze seemed to whisper, *don't be such a tight-ass!*

Aidan jerked so hard he nearly lost his balance. But a moment later Winnie's voice replaced his wife's, a voice every bit as strong and determined—even in pleading—as June's had been, along with a pair of smoky blue eyes unafraid to meet his dead-on. Of course, the woman was bleedin' crazy….

And sometimes crazy's just courageous in disguise.

June again. His nostrils flaring as he sucked in a deep breath, Aidan squeezed shut his eyes, remembering how June had said, after they'd met Winnie, how much alike she thought she and Winnie were.

"You couldn't be more wrong," Aidan said aloud, then shook his head, thinking, *And who's crazy now?* Only to violently shiver when the wind shoved at his back, insistent as a pair of hands, pushing him upright. Even more alarming was the way it seemed to be whistling, *Talk to her.* Just that, over and over, until he thought he'd go mad. Madder than he suspected he already was, at least.

The wind—and the whistling, and the words—stopped when he went back inside. *Thank God for small favors,* Aidan thought as he tossed his bottle in the garbage, then went upstairs to say good-night to his son. Except Robbie was already asleep, a tangle of bedclothes and long arms and legs, Spider-Man and Transformers at war. Aidan straightened out boy and bedding as best he could, then eased himself onto the edge of Robbie's bed to brush one permanently oil-paint-stained hand over his son's shaggy hair. And underneath the hair, a face that spoke the truth far more in sleep than it ever did when the lad was awake, his expression as tangled as his bedding.

"We're a right mess, you and I," Aidan said softly, the emptiness inside about to stretch him to bursting. Things were supposed to get easier, "they" said, after a year. Certainly, Aidan had hoped they'd be more adjusted to their new reality better than they apparently were.

Then he thought of the look in Winnie's eyes and realized that some realities are harder to adjust to than others, whether you're "supposed" to or not.

Aidan's loss was permanent, irreversible, the hopelessness of it an odd sort of comfort, he supposed. But for a nine-year-old child…

For a woman who, nine years ago, had quite possibly felt backed into a corner…

Releasing a long, silent sigh, Aidan rose from the bed and left his son's room, pulling his cell phone out of his pocket as he went.

Chapter Three

The next morning, Winnie awoke with a yelp when an ice-cold doggy nose torpedoed underneath the comforter to make contact with her warm back. Instantly awake—and cranky—Winnie flipped over to glare at the beast whose toothy grin was a blur in the wriggling excitement that was Annabelle.

It's morning? We go play? Find things to herd?

"Forget it," Winnie grumbled. Between feeling like she'd hosted a rowdy keg party in her brain all night and an unfamiliar bed, she was lucky if she'd logged in three hours the entire night. Morning, whatever. And it was coollld out there on the other side of the comforter—

"Oh, hell," she muttered, remembering that Aidan had invited her to breakfast. That she'd said yes. That loneliness and butter-soft Irish accents were a really, really bad combination. That—

That somewhere in the distance, a rooster was crowing.

"Crap, what time is it?" she asked the world at large, grabbing her watch off the nightstand, then sinking back into the mattress, groaning. *Lord, show me a sign,* she'd prayed the night before, mainly because Elektra was a big believer in the suckers and Winnie was up the creek, *whether I should go or stay.* Whether her wanting to get to know Robbie was a right idea, or a relapse into the stubbornness that had ruled so many decisions for so many years. Then Aidan had called, not a minute afterward, and she'd thought, *Wow. Fast service.*

"I can't do this," she now said to the dog, even though she had no earthly idea what *this* was. Annabelle stopped wriggling long enough to cock her head at her mistress, after which she heaved a great doggy sigh, laid her snout on top of the mattress and commiserated with Winnie with what she probably thought was her best soulful look. Except Annabelle, not being a hound, didn't do soulful very well. Annabelle was all about perky and playful. Like a cheerleader.

Sure enough, after, oh, ten seconds of sympathy, the dog moonwalked backward, bowed with her butt in the air and yarped. Her version of *Get your fat bee-hind out of bed. Now.*

With a sigh of her own, Winnie dragged said bee-hind out of bed, the comforter wrapped around her shoulders and trailing after her like a poufy coronation cape as she let the dog out, then clumsily put on coffee, because facing the world—and Aidan—without fresh caffeine in her system wasn't gonna happen.

Her cell rang. Winnie stared at it, shimmying on the counter like a rattlesnake, a thought that made her shudder mightily. With any luck, it would be Aidan, canceling. Except then she realized, yeah, well, if she wanted to get closer to Robbie, going through Aidan was her only option.

And according to Elektra, once you accepted a sign, you were pretty much stuck with it.

"Good," Aidan said the moment Winnie put her phone to her ear. Now she heard the crowing in stereo. "You're awake."

"Up, yes," she said, yawning. "Awake, not so much." Annabelle whined at the back door; Winnie shuffled over to let her in.

"I thought I said breakfast was at eight-t'irty?"

And early morning Irish attitude was just what she needed. "It's eight…" She squinted at her watch. "Ten. So no problem.'

"Glad to hear it," Aidan said, and hung up.

Winnie looked at Annabelle, who'd been pretending not to listen. "Tell me I'm doing the right thing," she said, but, sadly, dispensing advice was not part of Annabelle's job description.

The village of Tierra Rosa, Winnie thought as her truck wound up, then down, the curved main drag like a roller coaster on downers, was oddly charming, in a Tim-Burton-gone-Southwest kind of way—a cross between an old Spanish settlement, a set for a fifties' Hollywood Western and a trailer park. To add to the confusion, she mused as she spotted the cafe, was the occasional bank or church or police department building that was pure Sixties blah.

"No, baby," she said to the dog as she got out, leaving the truck windows at half-mast since the temperature had inched up to maybe fifty or so, "you have to stay here." After a moment of looking bereft, the dog sighed and sat. Annabelle was nothing if not flexible.

Then, the breeze zipping right through the persimmon-colored velvet blazer that had seen her through any number of Octobers, Winnie started toward the cafe and was hit by a wave of nervousness so strong she half expected to pass out. The moment she pushed through the glass door, however, the pungent aromas of coffee and griddle grease, the sounds of breakfast orders being barked to the cook, the crush of animated early-morning conversation, wrapped around her, both soothing and unsettling in their familiarity.

The place was nearly full, patrons squeezed around a half-dozen randomly placed tables, into as many bright-red booths. Hand-painted bougainvillea vines snaked underneath a heavily beamed ceiling, the bright pink flowers vibrating against deep-blue walls. The kitchen was open to the dining room, framed by an enormous mural depicting vintage pickups traveling along piñon-dotted mountains.

Nope, definitely not in Texas anymore, she thought, recovering from the onslaught of color. Her nostrils flared at the top note of roasted chili peppers seasoning every deep, calming breath, like Elektra had taught her before she gave birth, although as Winnie recalled when the time came they didn't do her a damn bit of good. Then her gaze snagged on Aidan, rising out of his chair, and she thought, *Not gonna do a damn bit of good now, either.*

He dwarfed the tiny table in front of him, the light streaming in through the window beside it bouncing off all those angles and muscles and things practically hard enough to *hear,* making his white shirt—open one button too far—downright glow. Some people might think the jeans rode a trifle too low, too. Winnie couldn't decide if she was one of those people or not.

Aidan angled his head slightly, his frown only accentuating the Celtic warrior/cowboy thing he had going with the wild hair, the beard shadow. Not that he was scuzzy—oh, my, no—but he was—

"If you don't mind?" he said, the frown deepening.

Sorely in need of some manners, Winnie thought irritably, winnowing her way through the maze of tables and chairs toward him, remembering why she was here. Reminding herself that Aidan had the upper hand. And that if she'd had any sense she would've left her hormones back in the truck with the dog.

However, the closer she got, the more she could see past the muscles and the too-low jeans and the sheer oh-my-*God*-ness of the man to the pain-pretending-to-be-annoyance in his eyes. A look she'd seen plenty, in various permutations, over the years as she'd poured yet another cup of coffee or set down a piece of pie or a serving of fresh-made meat loaf and whipped potatoes and gravy. This realization did not make her less nervous, exactly, as much as it somehow gave it a different color.

Although she somehow doubted she'd look back on her years of indentured servitude to her grandmother with anything resembling fondness, there was nothing like working in a diner to hone a person's ability to read people. The men, especially, hard-wired to believe they were impervious to things like sorrow and heartbreak.

She'd even been able to dispense the odd parcel of advice, now and then, when she'd known enough of the particulars to feel on sure footing. But this time, when something too formless to be a real thought suggested she might be able to help Aidan, too, she nearly laughed. Not only did she know nothing about the man, but how in heaven's name was she supposed to help somebody else when her own life felt about as solid as a half-set Jell-O salad?

Except then it felt like a pair of hands gently pushed her into the seat in front of him, and she sighed, resigning herself to this being one of those times when the angel-thought said, *Do this,* and you said, *Okay, I'll try.*

"You look different," Aidan said, like it was gonna bug him to no end until he figured out why.

Suddenly ravenous, Winnie picked up the laminated menu with hands she refused to let shake and said, "It's daylight."

"No, it's not that, it's…you're wearing makeup."

Winnie batted her eyes over the top of the menu. "So?"

"You weren't last night."

She shrugged. "End of the day. And I wasn't expecting company." Which wasn't exactly true, but whatever. "Trust me," she said, scanning the column of breakfast specials, "I'm doin' you a favor. But good news—no bunnies were harmed in the making of this mascara." Her selection made, she slammed down the menu. "So. What made you change your mind?" she said, taking no small pleasure in the look of surprise that crossed his features, just as the waitress— small, blond, fine-featured, grinning—appeared.

"Hey, Aidan…haven't seen you in here for a while."

"No, I suppose not," he said, not returning her smile, and Winnie briefly considered kicking him under the table. Except then the blonde gave Winnie a bemused shrug and a "watcha gonna do?" eye roll. And a light smack on Aidan's shoulder with her order pad. She was still young enough to look good under fluorescent lighting—and in tight black jeans—but old enough to smack ornery custom- ers with her order pad. Winnie liked her immediately.

"You gonna introduce me or what?"

Aidan frowned at Winnie. Like it had just occurred to him that maybe taking her someplace where people knew him hadn't been the smoothest move in the book.

"Thea, this is Winnie Porter. Winnie, Thea. Are the eggs fresh?"

"Considering they came from your chickens, I assume so. Salsa's fresh-made, too."

Aidan waited until after she'd taken their order and zipped back to the kitchen before he finally said, "What makes you think I've changed my mind?"

"Other than you giving the definite impression last night that you were hoping the mother ship would snatch me up?"

"That's assuming they'd be interested in reclaiming you."

"Brother. Your wife was clearly a saint."

"No argument there," Aidan muttered, his gaze drifting

outside as he sipped his coffee. He appeared to be looking at Annabelle, who was looking back. Winnie waved and the dog barked, although you couldn't really hear it through the glass. Then Aidan said, "Even so, I'm sorry I came down s'hard on you," and her gaze swung back to his.

But only for a moment. "You had cause," she said, lowering her eyes to spread her napkin on her lap, then upending the sugar dispenser over her coffee, watching the stream of white crystals disappear into the lake of dark, steaming liquid. Frankly, she needed more caffeine like a hole in the head, this being her third cup in less than an hour, but some days were like that.

She set the sugar dispenser back between them, stirred her coffee. "So, what?" she said, forcing herself to meet his gaze, aching for him whether she wanted to or not. "Is this some kind of trial? The number of correct answers determine whether I get to see Robbie or not?"

"It's not that cut-and-dried," he said, looking none too comfortable himself.

"No," Winnie said, lifting the heavy cup and taking a sip. Grimacing, she added more sugar. "I suppose not."

Her gaze drifted out to Annabelle again, lending her silent, but unwavering, support, her eyes cutting back to his when he said, "I gather my housekeeper paid you a little visit last night."

"She did." Winnie took another swallow of coffee. "Did I pass muster?"

"For having *cojones?* Yes. What's so funny?"

"Never heard that word with an Irish accent, that's all. But tell her thank you."

"That doesn't mean she's necessarily on your side."

"Tell me something I don't know." When Aidan's brows lifted, she said, "Flo's obviously very loyal to you. All of you," she added, backing up slightly when Thea brought them their food, then left to chat up a good-looking cowboy who'd just come in to pick up a take-out order, or so it looked like. She was all smiles; he wasn't, doing the whole eye-avoidance thing that spelled doom with a capital D, and Winnie, who'd been on the receiving end of that little scenario more times than she could count, thought, *Uh-oh.* Then he left, shoulders hunched with apology, and Thea's eyes touched Winnie's, full of hurt and confusion and embarrassment, before she disappeared through the archway marked Restrooms.

"That she is," Aidan said, and Winnie thought, *What? Oh. Flo. Right.*

She dug into her fried potatoes. "Which is how it should be. So it wasn't like I was sensing any real support from that camp. Still, I'm a big believer in fate."

Aidan paused, his fork suspended over his own *huevos rancheros.* "Willing something to happen isn't the same thing as fate."

Again, Winnie laughed, the food too good to stop eating. "Oh, honey…believe me, you'd know if I was being willful. This doesn't even come close." She leaned forward to butter a piece of toast, thinking that sometimes nothing hits the spot like a perfectly toasted piece of white bread drenched in butter. "And anyway, nobody told you to call me."

His eyes dipped to his breakfast, but not fast enough for her to miss his blush. "So this is my doing, is it?"

"Works for me."

Apparently stymied, at least for the moment, Aidan seemed unable to tear his gaze away from Winnie's slathering her omelet with copious amounts of thick, fragrant salsa.

"You might want t'go a little easy with that. It's not for wimps."

"I think I can handle it," she said, thinking maybe she was talking about more than salsa. She forked in a large bite of eggs—the stuff definitely had a kick, but she'd had hotter. "And you know, if this really is about gettin' to know me, you'll have to take at least some of it on face value, since it's not like I've got a half-dozen character witnesses in my back pocket. But I swear, I didn't come here to mess with anybody's head." The salsa hit the pit of her stomach with a small explosion. "Least of all Robbie's. And I also swear…"

"What?"

Winnie chewed for a moment, thinking that while she could probably B.S. her way through this little interview, in the long run what would be the point?

"Okay," she said, noting that Aidan seemed suitably impressed that she hadn't sucked down half a glass of water to douse the flames, "this probably isn't gonna earn me any points, seeing as you already think I'm a couple bricks shy of a load as it is. But since you brought up the whole human will thing? I didn't exactly *decide* to come out here."

"What you said about not having any family left notwithstanding."

"Oh, that was—is—true enough. Only that alone wouldn't've been enough to make me do something like this. But a couple days after my grandmother died…" She blew out a breath. "It was almost like I heard…a voice. Although not a *voice,* voice, more like…a real strong feeling. That I *had* to come here." At his what-kind-of-fool-do-you-take-me-for? expression, she shrugged. "I know. Elektra thought I was nuts, too. So there's another tick mark in your column."

"Elektra?"

"She runs my grandmother's diner. My diner now, I guess."

"You don't sound exactly thrilled."

"Yeah, well, it's not like I just inherited a chain of five-star hotels or anything. And I know I should be grateful. It'll never make me rich, but that's okay, I wouldn't know what to do with rich if it bit me in the butt. It's just not…me."

"And what is…you?" he asked, unsmiling.

"I think maybe I want to work with kids—I've got my teaching degree, I just have to get certified—but I haven't had five minutes to myself to think about it." Then she let out a sound that was equal parts laugh and sigh. "And here I'm supposed to be at least *trying* to make a decent impression. But you know what? I am who I am, either you deal with that or you don't. I may be a bit on the flaky side, but I'm not a bad person. Not anymore."

"Anymore?"

"Oh, come on—when we met, I'm sure I must've looked like I had the devil's mark on me. I sure felt that way at times. Although," she said, waving her fork, "I was not a rebel without a cause. Or at least a reason."

"You got pregnant on purpose?"

At least he looked more intrigued than judgmental, for what that was worth. "If I say I'm not sure," Winnie said, "it's not because I'm trying to evade the question, okay? It's because after all this time I still don't know." Frowning, she finally took that sip of water, then met his gaze. "Mostly I wanted to make my own decisions, about my own life. Even if they were stupid. But I'm not that person anymore, Aidan, you've got to believe that." She sucked in a long, shuddering breath. "I swear."

The tremor of sympathy happened before Aidan could squelch it. Oh, he definitely remembered the Winnie from back then, those big blue eyes bleeding a mixture of anger and fear and resentment. But most of all, an unfathomable sadness that, even then, had burned something inside Aidan. He remembered how wrong it had felt, that his and June's happiness should be predicated on someone else's misery.

"And how, exactly, d'you think you've changed?"

"Well…for one thing," she said after a moment, "I've stopped making myself the victim of my own anger. Took a while, though, before it finally dawned on me that trying to hurt somebody else is a surefire way of hurting yourself more. But until I got to that point…" She stared at her plate, her breathing hard, and Aidan waited out the next wave of sympathy. "Who knew it would be so much harder to love myself than my grandmother?"

"She didn't exactly strike me as the warm fuzzy type," Aidan said quietly, and Winnie snorted.

"That's what fear'll do to a person, I suppose. She was so afraid I'd go off half-cocked like she was convinced my mother did. Ida couldn't help being strict, that's just how she was raised herself. But every time she said…" Her face tilted toward the window; Aidan saw her swallow. "Every time she said, 'You're just like your mother,' the more I figured, what the hell, she already thinks the worst of me, might as well live up to her expectations."

Aidan's stomach clenched. "And what did she mean by that? Your being just like your mother?"

Winnie's mouth curved into a wry smile. "I gathered Mama was stubborn as all get-out, too. She apparently bucked my grandmother every chance she got, the crowning touch being to elope with my father the second she turned eighteen." Her eyes veered to Aidan's. "I remember Daddy being a good man. Kind. He just wasn't real successful, if you get my drift. I'm sure Ida saw Mama's 'bad choice' as her own failure, but growing up, all I knew was that my grandmother constantly bad-mouthed the people I'd loved most in the world. It didn't sit well."

Their breakfasts and their surroundings all but forgotten, Aidan caught himself a split second before he stumbled head-on into the now dry-eyed gaze in front of him. While he knew Winnie wasn't playing him for a con, anger still swamped him with an intensity bordering on painful.

He didn't want to feel sympathy for Winnie Porter or anybody else, dammit, didn't want to get sucked into anybody else's sad tale. Not now, not ever again. June had been the compassionate one in the marriage, the one with the bottomless heart. But while Aidan had loved his wife beyond measure, and would do anything for his son...

Refusing to even finish the thought, he jabbed a fork into his now cold eggs. "Your antipathy sounds completely justified to me."

"Maybe. But even I realized it wasn't healthy. By the time Ida got sick, I'd come to terms with a thing or two. At least, I learned to channel the anger in more positive ways."

"You forgave her?"

Winnie sighed. "The resentment gets to be a real bitch to lug around, you know? Her wanting more for my mother wasn't a bad thing in itself. And I know it nearly killed her when Mama died. God knows it was no fun living with a woman who tended her disappointment and heartache like some prize orchid, but it wasn't her fault she got sick. And if nothing else, I sure learned a lot from her example."

"And what's that?"

"Not to take out your own pain on anybody else. Least of all an innocent child."

After a long moment, Aidan said, indicating her now empty plate, "Are you done?" When Winnie nodded, he signaled for Thea, pulling his credit card out of his wallet when she gave him the bill. "I suppose you think I'm being a hardnose by not wanting Robbie to know who you are."

Winnie wiped her mouth on her napkin, demolishing what was left of her light-colored lipstick. "You're his father, Aidan," she said at last. "Like you said, I gave up any right to a say in the matter a long time ago, and I have to trust that you know what's best for your own son."

"And has it occurred to you," Aidan bit out, "that since he's already seen you, already knows you're staying on our property, what might happen if and when he does ask about you down the road? You've put me in an untenable position, Winnie. You do realize that, don't you?"

Her cheeks flushed scarlet. "I'm so sorry," she muttered, getting up and grabbing her purse from the floor. "Here I'm telling you how far I've come, about learning that's it not all about me, and then I go and do exactly the same thing I've always done." She straightened, swiping a stray piece of hair out of her eyes as a markedly less bubbly Thea set the charge slip in front of Aidan. "All I wanted…" Shaking her head, she backed away, stumbling into an empty chair before turning and striding toward the door.

A sane man would have let her go, with her earnestness and regret and those damnably soulful eyes. Eyes that had shaken him nine years ago, even when he'd been happy and in love and she'd been little more than the means to his becoming a father. Ashamed, angry, Aidan scribbled his signature on the slip and took off after her. Already to her truck, she turned at his approach, her gaze wary. Embarrassed. He stopped a few feet away, breathing hard. Annoyed as all hell.

"Okay, look," he said, determined to keep the blame for this whole mess firmly at her feet, "I still think the timing sucks, that tellin' Robbie the truth right now…" The very thought made him ache, even if he couldn't completely define the "why" behind it. "But maybe…"

Turning slightly to dodge the hope in her eyes, Aidan felt the ends of his too-long hair whip at his face. "Maybe if he got to know you a little first, we could somehow ease him into it."

After too many beats passed, he looked at Winnie again. She was frowning, holding her own wind-blown hair out of her face.

"You sure about this?"

"Not a'tall."

Her expression didn't change. "What you really want is for me to say I've changed my mind, isn't it?"

"You have no idea."

She looked away then, frowning, then back at him. "I promise, I won't tell him. Not until you give the go-ahead."

"Come to supper tonight, then," he said, feeling the none-too-solid ground he'd been navigating for the past year give way a bit more. "Around seven. Just follow the road up from the Old House. And keep an eye out for the chickens."

An amused expression crossed her features before settling back into concern. "What are you going to tell him? About why I'm there?"

"I've no idea. I suppose I'll figure something out."

She nodded, then opened her door. Hugging the shimmying dog, she angled her head enough to say, "Thank you."

But Aidan didn't want her thanks. He didn't want any of this, not the responsibility or the sympathy those damn blue eyes provoked or…any of it. Most of all, he didn't want to be nice or kind or even civil unless absolutely necessary. So he spun around and strode to his own truck, parked on the other side of the small lot, thinking that she'd been dead wrong, about needing makeup in the daylight.

"So that's the update," Winnie said to Elektra later, leaning against her truck's bumper, watching her credit-card bill soar as the little numbers flicked by on the gas pump faster'n she could read 'em. Her nerves much too frayed to go back to the little house and sit there staring into space, Winnie had instead decided to do some sight-seeing, immediately nixing Santa Fe—very pretty, way too crowded with looky-loos for her and Annabelle's taste—for a nice, long meander along the back roads connecting any number of little towns like Tierra Rosa. The weather was almost embarrassingly gorgeous, the views of endless blue sky and color-splotched mountains definitely spirit-lifting. Not to mention head-clearing.

"Huh," Elektra said, adding, "Hold on, baby." Following the whirring of the credit card machine, Winnie heard E's "Y'all have a safe trip, okay?" before she came back on the horn. "So tell me something…would you have gone out there if you'd've known June had passed?"

"I don't know," Winnie sighed out, frowning as the pump kept going…and going…and going… "All I know is, whatever's gonna happen tonight, is gonna happen. Robbie and I are either gonna click or we won't."

Silence. "You *could* leave."

"No," Winnie said quietly. "I can't. Not now." When a great sigh sailed over the line, she said, "Aidan's right, E—Robbie's a lot less likely to freak when he finds out who I am if he already likes me. Right?" The pump finally stopped, exhausted; blowing out a relieved sigh of her own, Winnie plugged the nozzle back into place and took her receipt, not having the courage to look at it. She got back into her truck, dodging Annabelle's kisses. Would she could do the same to Elektra's heavy, meaningful silence. "It'll be okay, E," she said.

"Uh-huh. And maybe this'll be the week I finally win the lottery."

"Maybe it will, you never know. Gotta go," Winnie said over the old engine's growl. "They're really serious about no driving while using a cell up here—"

"Baby?"

"Yeah?"

A pause. Then: "Be careful."

I am, dammit, Winnie thought, tires crunching gravel as she pulled onto the road leading into Tierra Rosa, even as another voice snorted, *Like hell.*

"Who asked you?" she muttered.

Twenty minutes later she was back in town; starving, she swung by Garcia's, to be greeted by a still perky but slightly subdued Thea.

"Well, hey, again…Winnie, right? What can I get you?"

"Steak and cheese burrito to go." Thea yelled her order toward the kitchen, then turned back, questions blatant in amber eyes as Winnie paid. Ignoring them, she instead looked around.

"Great place."

"Thanks. Not that I can take any credit, I just work here."

A customer came up to the register to pay; Winnie noticed the blonde's hands were shaking when she made change from the twenty. When he'd left, Winnie leaned in and whispered, "You okay?" and Thea's eyes snapped to hers. "It's just I couldn't help noticing this morning…" She felt her face warm. "None of my business, sorry."

"No, it's okay, I'm…touched that you cared enough to ask. Not that I'm gonna unload on a complete stranger, but…" Her mouth curved. "Thanks—"

"Thea! Order up!"

The waitress hurried to the rear to pick up Winnie's wrapped lunch, handing it over just as a couple came in, cutting off any chance of further conversation.

Just as well, probably, Winnie thought as she got back into the truck, fending off Annabelle, who was also partial to steak and cheese burritos. The plan had been to head straight back to the house for a nap that would hopefully make up for her lost sleep the night before. Not stop at the pumpkin patch she'd passed earlier. Except who could resist the afternoon sun blazing across pumpkins as far as the eye can see?

Certainly not her.

Now, what she thought she was gonna do with them, she thought a half hour later as she lugged a half dozen of the suckers out of her truck bed, she had no idea. Especially considering she'd be back in Texas long before Halloween. And, once she'd rearranged them several times on the porch until she and Annabelle were satisfied, she realized they clashed terribly with the bright pink cosmos. Still,

Winnie had always been impressed with how things could work together in nature that you could never pull off in, say, your own house. Or on your body, she thought with a grimace, recalling more than one unfortunate outfit she'd thought the very height of fashion at the time.

A breeze whooshed through the trees, like a soft laugh. Winnie took a deep breath, than another, letting the wind suck the tension right out of her, as she decided the earthy orange and purply pink actually looked pretty damn good with the vibrant blue trim on the doors and windows. So there.

At last she wolfed down her burrito, chasing it with a glass of milk, then collapsed across the unmade bed, barely kicking off her boots before she'd passed out. And who knows how long she might have slept if somebody hadn't knocked on the door, maybe an hour later. Finger-combing her hair and trying to shake off the dregs of sleep, Winnie plodded in socks to the door, just as whoever was on the other side knocked again. A lightish knock, not the pounding one might expect from, say, a six-foot-something grumpy Irishman.

Throwing caution to the winds, she swung open the door to face a very disgruntled nine-year-old in a dusty hoodie standing on the porch, his bike collapsed in the dirt a few feet away.

"So who are you, anyway?" Robbie said, with the exasperation of somebody who'd been thinking about this for some time.

Chapter Four

Robbie didn't know why somebody staying in the Old House bugged him so much. Especially since the lady'd said she was only there for a week. And she seemed okay and all, when he'd met her in the store. But why was she staying *here?* He asked Flo, but she was no help. All Robbie knew was that the lady's being there felt worse than when Florita would come into his room without knocking.

Because this was where he could think about Mom all he wanted, sometimes even talk to her—even though he knew he wasn't *really* talking to her, he wasn't some dumb little kid who believed in ghosts—but he could say things to her he couldn't to Dad, like about how much he still missed her and stuff. It was even okay if he cried, because there was nobody around to see him. Of course he thought about Mom up at his real house, too, or when he was out walking in the woods or riding his bike, but this was different.

All day at school, he kept thinking about how it felt like

this lady was coming between him and Mom, even though he knew that was stupid. Poor Miss Carter, she'd had to tell him to focus like a million times.

So as soon as he got off the school bus, he decided to just go ask her himself. As soon as he did, though, he felt really dumb. Especially since the lady got this strange look on her face.

"My name's Winnie," she said, smiling and coming out onto the porch. She didn't shut the door behind her or anything, but Robbie still felt like he was being kept out, which made him mad. Only then she said, "I'd invite you inside, but I'm sure you know you shouldn't do that with a stranger," and it freaked him out, a little, that she'd kinda read his mind. "You're Robbie, right?"

He nodded, then said, "Why'd you come?"

"I saw a piece in a magazine about Tierra Rosa, and it looked so nice I decided to come see it for myself, and since you don't have any motels or anything—"

"I don't want you here," Robbie said, his face getting all hot; as he looked away, the dog came up to him and licked his hand, like she understood how bad he felt.

Instead of getting upset or mad, though, Winnie slipped her hands into her pockets. "This is your hideout, isn't it?"

Robbie's face got hotter. Ten times worse, though, was feeling like he was gonna cry. "Sorta."

"I didn't know," Winnie said softly, calling the dog to her. Not looking at him. "When I made arrangements to stay here, I mean. I had no idea this was your place." She got quiet for a moment, then said, "I won't be here long, though. I promise."

"You said a week, back at the store."

"I might leave sooner. I haven't decided yet."

Something in her face made Robbie feel like he was looking in a mirror, like she was as sad as he was, but trying real hard not to show it. Which made him feel bad, because it wasn't like her fault or anything. Then he noticed the pumpkins.

"If you're not gonna stay, how come you got all these pumpkins?"

Winnie laughed. "It was just one of those impulse things."

"What's that mean?"

"When you do something without thinking it through." She sighed, then ruffled the dog's fur. "I do that a lot. It's a bad habit."

Staring at the pumpkins, Robbie said, "Halloween useta be my mom's favorite holiday."

"Yeah? Mine, too."

"You gonna carve faces in 'em?"

"Probably. When I get back home, closer to Halloween. If I cut 'em now, they'll shrivel up too fast."

"Yeah, I know." He paused. "My mom died. Right before Halloween last year."

"Oh, honey…I'm so sorry," she said, like she really meant it. "My folks died, too, when I was about your age."

He looked at her, curious.

"How?"

"In a car crash," she said softly.

"Oh."

He'd never known anybody else whose parents had died when they were still a kid. Maybe that's why she didn't go all stupid and act all embarrassed and stuff like a lot of other people did, either treating him all fake nice or refusing to look right at him. Before he knew what he was doing, he sat on the step beside her. The dog brought him a stick to throw.

"What's her name?"

"Annabelle. Although sometimes I call her Dumbbell."

Robbie almost laughed. He threw the stick for the dog, then heard himself say, "When Mom was sick, I'd come here a lot."

"Just to be by yourself?"

"Yeah. And now it's almost like..."

"What?"

He shook his head. He couldn't believe he'd almost told her about feeling like Mom was here now. Like she'd moved into the Old House after she'd died. "Nothin'," he said, shrugging. "I forgot what I was about to say."

"I do that, too," Winnie said. Robbie looked at her.

"Yeah?"

"Yeah. Lots. It used to drive my grandmother crazy. She raised me after my parents died. She's dead, too, now. Hey—you want a banana? Or a granola bar? I mean, if you think it's okay."

"Yeah, it's okay." He thought. "Could I have both?"

"Sure," Winnie said, getting up, her voice kinda shaky when she told the dog to stay outside with Robbie.

Her eyes burning, Winnie collapsed against the wall next to the door, the plaster rough through her cotton top as she willed the shakes to stop. It wasn't supposed to be like this, she wasn't supposed to fall so hard, so fast...

Oh, for heaven's sake, girl, pull yourself together. Jerking in a sharp breath, she crossed to grab a couple of bananas and a granola bar off the table, then headed back outside. Half of her wished like hell her son would be gone, the other half...

The other half was laughing its fool head off.

Robbie had just tossed the stick for Annabelle again when she walked out onto the porch. He took the banana, started to peel it. Desperately trying for nonchalant, Winnie lowered herself beside him again, peeling her own, trying not to react to his innocent, dusty scent. The confusion seeping from his pores.

"Thanks," he said.

"You're welcome."

"You got any brothers or sisters or anybody?" he asked around a full mouth.

"Nope."

He looked at her. "You mean you're really all alone?" *Thanks, kid.* "I really am."

Robbie frowned at his banana for a moment, then took another bite. "I have a Mam and Pap in Ireland. That's what they call grandparents there. But I've only seen them a couple of times, and once was right after I was 'dopted, so that doesn't really count."

The damn fruit was burning a hole in her stomach. *Please don't say anything more about being adopted,* she prayed. *Please.* "It probably does for them."

"I guess." Robbie finished his banana, then ripped the wrapping off the granola bar. "Chocolate chips! Cool."

"You didn't strike me as a raisin kind of kid," Winnie said, laughing when he made a face.

Annabelle sat in front of them, polite but doleful. "Can I give her a piece?" Robbie asked.

"She'd be cool with it, but chocolate isn't good for dogs. So, no."

The child gnawed off the end of his bar, frowning. "You know what really sucks?"

Winnie held her breath. "What?"

"The way people keep all the time saying that Dad'll probably get married again some day, and then I'd have another mother." When he looked at her, she could see how close the tears were to falling, and her heart broke. "And how dumb is that?"

"Pretty dumb," she said, hoping he wouldn't notice how shiny her eyes probably were, too. "Because nobody can ever take your mom's place, right?"

"No *way.* I mean, when your mom died, did you ever think about having another one?"

Winnie shook her head. She'd been devastated when her

parents died, naturally, but after all this time it was more about remembering the pain, not feeling it. "Not that there would have been any chance of that, but…no."

"Dad would never marry somebody else. He's too sad. And anyway, Florita says he's such a grouch nobody else would have him."

The laugh popped out before she knew it was there. Still, she said, "Sometimes when people are really sad, they get angry. So your dad might not be like that forever." Then again, Aidan Black seemed to positively enjoy his crankiness, like a cup of good, hot coffee on a chilly day. She reached down to brush clay dust off her boot. "I bet your mom was a real special lady."

Robbie frowned. "Why do you think that? Did you know her?"

"No. But it takes a special mom to raise a special kid."

He frowned harder, almost comically. "You think I'm special?"

Dangerous ground, honey, she heard in her head. *Proceed with extreme caution.* "Well, I don't know *you* very well, either, but I'm pretty good at reading people."

"Reading people? Like a book?"

"Sort of. Except instead of reading words, I get these feelings about who people really are by watching their faces, listening to their voices, paying attention to how they act. I'm not always right, but mostly I am. And I'm guessing…" She looked at him with narrowed eyes, thinking, *Will you even remember this conversation a year from now? Will you remember the crazy lady with the hyperactive dog and too many pumpkins on her porch?* "That…you get in trouble sometimes, but never anything too serious. Just regular stuff, like most kids. That you probably do okay in school, but you like weekends better. That you still miss your mama a lot, but maybe…"

"What?"

"Never mind."

"No, seriously—what?"

His eyes were so blue, so earnest. So damn much like hers. "That maybe it's hard for you to tell your daddy how you feel?" When he turned away, she sighed and said, "I'm sorry, I probably shouldn't've said that. It's that impulsive thing again. Saying something without thinking it through?"

Robbie scrubbed one shoulder over his eyes. "No, it's okay." Then he squinted up into the trees, mumbled, "I gotta go," and sprang from the step and over to his fallen bike. He yanked it upright and straddled it. "C'n I come see you again tomorrow, maybe?"

Winnie folded her hands in front of her so tightly they hurt. "I thought you didn't want me here?"

The kid blushed. "I guess it's okay if you hang around."

"Oh. Wow. Thanks. But…" Her heart cowered. "I think I've changed my mind. So I'm probably leaving in the morning."

"But you'll come back, right?"

"Oh, sugar…" *Don't,* she thought, blinking back tears. *Don't…*

Slowly, she shook her head, startled out of her wits when a hurt, angry "Fine! Do whatever you want to!" exploded out of the kid's mouth, at the precise moment they both heard his father's barked, "Robbie! What in the devil's name are you doing here?"

Winnie jumped to her feet as Robbie started, just as Aidan emerged from the woods at the side of the house. And even through unshed tears, Winnie could tell he was one seriously pissed hombre.

Aidan barely caught Winnie's surreptitious swipe at her eyes before he refocused his attention on his son, who looked more confused than guilty.

"Nothin'. I just…" He glanced at Winnie, then back at Aidan. "I just wanted to find out who she was, that's all—"

"It's okay," Winnie started to say, but Aidan shot her a quelling look that, amazingly, actually shut her up. Then he looked back at Robbie.

"You *know* better than t'go anywhere without first checking in with Florita or me," he said quietly. "Flo was beside herself with worry. So you get yourself back up to the house, right now. And except to go to school, don't plan on leaving it for at least t'ree days."

"Dad!"

"Go on."

Grumbling, the lad took off; when he'd disappeared from sight, Winnie said, "That was a little harsh, wasn't it?"

Aidan pivoted, almost grateful for a reason to be angry with her. "For breaking the one rule Junie and I insisted on from the time he could walk? I don't think so. And where d'you get off criticizing my decisions?"

She dug in her pants pocket for a tissue, blew her nose. "Sorry," she mumbled into the tissue, then crossed her arms. "You're right, it's not my place. Although if you notice I didn't say anything in front of R-Robbie."

Aidan looked away. "I suppose I should be grateful for that, at least."

"Yes, you should," she said, sounding stronger. "I swear I had no idea you didn't know where he was—"

"And didja think I would have *allowed* him to come here?"

"How the hell should I know, Mr. Come Up to the House For Dinner Tonight—?"

"Didja tell him?"

"That I was his birth mother? Of course not," she said in the manner of a woman who's had it up to *here*. "I'm not *that* stupid. Or selfish. *Or* a liar. I said I wouldn't say anything, and I didn't. Besides, if I had, don't you think that would've been the first thing out of his mouth when he saw you?"

"But he said—"

"He asked who I was. So I told him my name, I didn't figure that could hurt anything. Especially since you told me he didn't know." Although she appeared to have recovered her equilibrium, her body language positively screamed her turmoil. An intuition confirmed when she added, "Maybe dinner tonight's not such a good idea."

"And here you'd sworn you'd changed," Aidan said over an unaccountable surge of anger.

Her eyes widened, until, suddenly, he saw realization dawn. "I honestly didn't think I'd feel any real connection," she said in quiet amazement, looking away. "Not after all these years. And certainly not after two short conversations." She swiped a hand across her nose. "So, yeah, I guess I'm right back where I was eight and a half years ago." Her eyes veered to his. "He's a really great kid."

Aidan swallowed. "You can thank June for that."

She studied him for such a long time his face began to heat. "I wish I'd known her better."

"You had your chance."

"I know," Winnie said softly, then released a breath. "I'm leaving in the morning. I won't bother you again."

The rush of relief wasn't nearly as sweet as he might have expected. But then, nothing was these days. And probably never would be again, he thought as she added, "If Robbie wants to see me when he's older—"

"How will you explain?"

"That we've already met? I don't know." She forked her bangs off her forehead. "If I'm lucky, maybe it won't matter by then." A chagrined half smile touched her mouth. "Sorry for the trouble."

Unable to speak for reasons he couldn't fully explain, Aidan simply nodded, then turned toward the path. He'd been so thrown, when he'd discovered Robbie'd gone missing, that he'd taken off on foot without thinking. Now he faced one helluva hike back up the mountain—

He frowned, noticing the pumpkins lined up on the porch. Not as many as June would have gathered, but enough to prick the treacherously thin membrane containing the memories. He twisted back around. "Did Robbie say anything else? Aside from asking who you were?"

Winnie gave him a strange look. "I don't know what you mean."

"Neither do I, really. It's just…I don't know what he's thinking anymore—"

The words had fallen from his mouth without his brain even giving a nod of approval. As if Winnie herself had somehow pulled them out of him. But that was crazy. Impossible. His gaze shifted again to the pumpkins, glowing in the last rush of daylight, and he could have sworn he saw faces in them already. Or at least, one face in particular—

"If you want to know what we talked about," Winnie said softly, "maybe you should ask him yourself." Then she disappeared inside the house before he could say, *Have a safe trip.*

Not that he would have, but he would have liked the chance.

That distant rooster's crow keeping her company, Winnie thunked yet another pumpkin into the truck bed the next morning, her stomach none too chipper about the carton of Snickers ice cream she'd forced into it the night before in some lame attempt to staunch the ache. And not just for herself, or even the child she'd given up the right to call her son years before, but for the agony in Aidan's eyes. The fear, that having already lost his wife, he might lose his child, as well.

Even if she doubted he knew that's what he was feeling.

But he was definitely aware of the communication breakdown. He just didn't know what to do about it.

Oh, and like you do?

Winnie sighed. Okay, that wasn't entirely true. She supposed she could call the man and say, "Two words: family counseling." And she might yet…once she crossed the Texas border. Even so, whatever these people needed, she wasn't the one to supply it. And not only because her timing couldn't have been worse, but also because…

Because she couldn't handle it.

Just like she hadn't been able to handle it before, when she'd backed out of their arrangement. Aidan was right, she hadn't changed at all. Or *a'tall,* as he might say.

She'd been half tempted to toss everything into the truck and take off right then and there, until reason prevailed and she realized she was far too emotionally drained for the long drive back, especially at night. Although—breathing hard, she glared at the thirty-pound monster pumpkin still on the porch, decided *Forget it*—considering how badly she'd slept again, she might as well have left last night. If she had—

"C'mon, girl," she called to the dog, then climbed up behind the steering wheel after her.

—she'd be home by now. Home, with all this craziness behind her—

"What the heck?" she muttered when she turned the ignition key and got…nothing. Not a growl, not a rumble, not even a burp.

She tried again. Still nothing.

Her eyes shut, Winnie slumped back in her seat. Muttering bad words. While she wasn't the most mechanically inclined chick in the world, even she knew a dead battery when she heard it. Or in this case, didn't hear it. But how could that be? She'd just had a tune-up before the trip, she hadn't left the lights on or anything….

So much for her dramatic exit. Okay, not so dramatic, it

wasn't like she had any witnesses, except for the pumpkins and the dog. But still. In her head, it had been dramatic.

On a weary sigh, Winnie fished her phone out of her shirt pocket and punched in Aidan's cell number. Nothing there, either, not even voice mail. The man truly took reclusiveness to new heights. And she had no clue what his house phone was, or if he even had a landline.

On another, even wearier sigh, she banged open her truck door, slid to the ground, waited for the dog, then began what turned out to be a surprisingly long trek up the leaf-strewn dirt road, the crowing growing louder with each step.

Chapter Five

"Day-um," Winnie muttered twenty long, panting minutes later, when she came upon the multilevel, timber-and-glass-and-tin-roof mountain hideaway set in the fowl-infested clearing, every surface either blending into or reflecting its surroundings. *Not the place to be in case of a forest fire,* she thought over the frenzied clucking of chickens with a Border collie in their midst, followed closely by, *Then again, some things are worth the risk.*

And standing here gawking at it wasn't getting her home.

She and Annabelle waded through the chickens—well, Winnie waded; Annabelle did her slinking herding thing, only to discover that chickens didn't herd—then climbed the stone steps leading up to the wide-planked porch. Winnie pressed the doorbell, twisting to admire the incredible view while she waited for Florita to answer. A few seconds later, she heard the door open behind her, followed by a chilly pause.

She turned. Not Florita.

"You have chickens?"

"Flo has chickens," Aidan grumbled.

"Speaking of whom… Where is she?"

"Out. Took her niece shopping."

"Tess? The one who's pregnant—?"

"What do you want?"

"Not a morning person, are we?" Aidan glowered at her. Winnie sighed, trying not to notice how well his paint-smeared, waffle-weave Henley clung to his torso. That his hair was still damp from his shower, all cherub-curly around his anything-but-cherubic features. That apparently her hormones and his pheromones were a perfect match. "My car battery's dead," she said, holding her breath. "I need a phone book. Or the number of a mechanic."

"You don't belong to an auto club?"

"Since I never go anywhere—up until now, I mean—it didn't seem worth the expense."

"Did you leave your lights on?"

"No, I did not leave my lights on," she said, thinking, *What is this, twenty questions?* a split second before Aidan said, "So you jumped into your truck and drove all the way here without checking first to make sure everything was in working order?" and Winnie wondered if he had *any* idea how close she was to smacking him clear into next week.

"Okay, Aidan? This little detour was not on my agenda this morning, so I was already halfway to pissed when you opened the door. Of *course* I had the truck tuned up before I left. And the battery's new, I had it replaced before right before the trip, I have no idea why it's dead. So if you'd just hand me the phone book—"

"You walked all the way up here from the Old House?"

Apparently completely oblivious to her having just read him the riot act, Aidan was now squinting past Winnie's shoulder. Wondering what sort of fumes he'd been breathing over the years, she muttered, "Short of saddling Annabelle, that was my only option…. What are you doing?"

What he was doing was putting on a denim jacket and coming out onto the porch, closing the house door behind him. Then he kept going, turning when he got halfway down the porch steps to spit out, "Well? Are y'coming with me or not?"

She crossed her arms. "Excuse me—did I pass out for a second and miss a chunk of the conversation? Coming with you where?"

That got a put-upon sigh. "Back to your truck, of course."

"And…why are you taking me back to my truck?"

Another sigh. "So I can have a look myself?" At her continued blank stare, he added, "Before you go and t'row your money at some yahoo who'd be only too glad to take it from you for basically nothing?"

Apparently, the more agitated he became, the heavier his accent got. It was almost cute, in a remarkably irritating kind of way. "Somehow you don't strike me as the mechanical type."

"Looks can be deceivin'. Now can we get a move on? I haven't got all day."

"Oh, for God's sake—just give me the damn phone book so I can call a mechanic or somebody—"

"Don't know where t'is," Aidan said, continuing to his own truck.

On a sigh, Winnie followed.

Ten minutes later, the verdict was in.

"It's not your battery," came Aidan's half-muffled voice from in the bowels of her truck. "It's your alternator."

"Are you kidding me?" Against her better judgment, she got right up beside him to have a look, staring so hard into the netherworld under her truck's hood she could almost ignore the low, steady hormonal hum thrumming through her veins. Like getting too close to uranium with a Geiger counter. "So that's what killed my battery?"

"It would seem so."

Not that Winnie entirely knew what she was looking at, but at least she knew what an alternator was for. Of course, she knew what her kidneys were for, too, but she didn't know what they looked like, either. With her luck, it would probably be cheaper to get a new kidney.

As though reading her mind, Aidan said, "The good news is, I can change out both and save you a bundle." Although he didn't sound like this was exactly good news for *him*.

"And the bad news?"

He slammed shut her hood, wiping his hands on an old rag he'd had in his own truck. "What makes you think there's bad news?"

"Could be that dark cloud always hanging over your head."

He looked at her steadily for a long moment—tick! tick! *tickticktickticktick!*—then let out the sigh of a man whose patience is being sorely tried. "If we set out for Santa Fe now, we can pick up the parts and I can have you on your way after lunch."

"I hate to put you to so much trouble—"

"And we can stand here arguing for the rest of the mornin', or you can stop being so bloody stubborn and we can get goin'."

"Can Annabelle come, too?"

And yet another sigh. "Yes, Annabelle can come, too."

"You really can't wait until I'm gone, can you?" she said, reluctantly trooping around to the passenger side of his truck and climbing in. After Annabelle.

From behind the wheel, Aidan muttered, "Truer words were never spoken." And yanked the shift into Reverse.

* * *

You have no idea, Aidan thought as they pulled out onto the highway leading to Santa Fe, *how much I want you gone.* How much damage those big blue eyes, that smart mouth, were doing. He had never thought of himself as the protective type when it came to women, not even before he met June, who'd prided herself on her self-sufficiency. At first Aidan had assumed that June's being so much older than he accounted for her self-confidence, but the longer he knew her the more he realized that's simply who she was.

And it wasn't that Winnie was helpless, her obvious inability to pick a decent mechanic notwithstanding. Far from it. In fact, Aidan surmised that any man fool enough to play the Little Woman card with her would find both him and his card reduced to pulp. Still, there was something about the woman—

"You really know how to install a new battery and alternator?" she asked from the other side of the far-too-short bench seat.

—that would drive him completely 'round the bend before lunch, if he didn't keep his guard up.

"I really do." From the seat behind them, her dog groaned. "My mother's family's farmed for generations. By the time I was fourteen I was an old hand at fixing tractors and such. And anyway, when you live out in the sticks you learn to take care of your own t'ings, not count on somebody else to do it for you."

"Oh," she said, then fell silent, thinking her own thoughts, and Aidan realized with a punch to his gut that the stillness was much, more worse than her blathering.

Desperate to flatten the silence, he said, "So. What will you do when you get back?"

"Please don't feel obligated to make polite conversation," she said, wearily. "I know you're not really interested."

Her rebuke stung far more than he would have expected.

Even if she was dead-on in her assessment. "I'm sorry if I come across as somewhat...gruff. One of the hazards of keeping to myself so much." When she didn't reply, he stole a glance at her profile. "And that's the best I can do for an apology, so if you're expectin' more—"

"I'm not *expecting* anything, Aidan. I never was." She paused, then added, "I never do."

"Have you really had it that bad?" he said, and her head snapped around. After a moment, she shook it.

"No, actually," she said, suddenly guarded. "There's just...been a lot of disappointments along the way. A broken promise here, a broken heart there..."

A soft laugh preceded, "But, hey—I've got my dog, right? And I've got friends back home, and a house and a business...things could be a lot worse." She hesitated, then said, "For what it's worth, I think I'm an okay person. Should the subject ever arise with Robbie," she added when Aidan frowned at her. "I don't smoke, don't drink enough to count, don't cheat, don't gamble—at least, not with money—and when I say I'll do something, I do it. Like my degree—took me six years, but I did it."

"And you don't strike *me* as the academic sort."

Winnie snorted. "We're talkin' early childhood education, not a doctorate in advanced physics. Or obscure English authors of the eighteenth century. Not that it was a walk in the park. You have no idea the psychology classes you have to take, just to teach elementary school." She laughed again. "Little kids are so neat. And while I'm waiting on having my own—"

At her breath catch, Aidan's head swung around. But she lifted one hand in a clear attempt to ward off his concern.

"Sorry, that kinda took me by surprise. So. Let's talk about you."

"You already know everyt'ing y'need to know."

"If you mean that meeting with the lawyer nine years ago, I'm thinking an update's probably in order."

"And if your car hadn't broken down, you would've left without your 'update.' And probably none the worse for not getting it."

"True. But obviously I wasn't meant to go home this morning."

"It doesn't necessarily follow we were meant to bond."

"Ohmigosh. Was that an attempt at humor?"

"No."

She laughed. And Aidan sighed, because deep down he wasn't a bad person, either, just one who preferred his existence as complication-free as possible. So while he took some small pleasure in Winnie's better mood, he took none whatsoever in…all the rest of it.

"And here we are," he said, immensely grateful.

He pulled off the highway into the Auto Zone parking lot, fully aware of Winnie's smirk. They got out of the truck, their doors slamming shut in rapid-fire succession, Winnie striking out across the lot a few feet ahead. Aidan hustled to catch up, barely noticing the flash of red parking lights, the roar of the SUV's engine, a split second before the driver—clearly not paying attention—gunned the huge black monster backward.

"Jaysus!" he bellowed, hauling Winnie backward against his chest an instant before the tank-size vehicle would've flattened her. Bastard didn't even slow down.

"Are you all right?" he said in Winnie's ear, her heart pounding against his arm where he still held her fast across her ribs, her scent storming the gates of his self-preservation, and through the rush of adrenaline a memory whispered, over his skin, through his blood.

"Yeah, I'm fine," she said on a rush of air. A beat passed. "You can let go now."

He did; setting herself to rights—a tug here, an adjustment there—Winnie glared in the direction of the vanished car. "Dirtwad," she muttered, then continued toward the entrance. Except she suddenly spun on Aidan and said, "You are *such* a phony," and he said, "What?" and she said, with much gesticulating, "You might talk tough and all, do the whole *I don't give a damn about people* routine, like that's supposed to scare people off." She yanked open the store's door before he could do it for her. "Except anybody with two eyes in their head can see it's all just *a great big act.*"

Inexplicably furious, Aidan grabbed Winnie's arm as soon as they were inside. She whirled around, her expression a combination of irritation and curiosity. But fear? Not a bit of it.

"Believe me," he snapped, his own heart pounding five times harder than hers had a moment ago, "I give a damn. About Robbie, about the people who matter to me. Just because I prefer to keep that circle small doesn't mean I don't care about the people who are in it." He let her go. "Is that clear?"

Their gazes tangled for several seconds before, wordlessly, she headed toward the counter in back. And as she did, Aidan became acutely aware that every set of male eyes in the place veered to her like divining rods.

His forehead knotting, he tried desperately to see what they found so damned interesting and failed miserably. Yes, he supposed she had a way of moving that was somewhat…arresting. And what man in his right mind wouldn't notice her hair, shiny as wet paint beneath the lights? Or the way her worn jeans cupped her legs and bottom below that soft as cream velvet jacket? But aside from that…Winnie was nothing extraordinary. Certainly not the kind of woman to make a man's eyes bug out.

And certainly there was absolutely no reason whatsoever for the bizarre spike of jealousy whenever one of the local yokels gave her the eye.

Oddly, she had no problem with telling the balding, potbellied clerk exactly what they needed. To the man's credit, he at least waited until Winnie's gaze drifted elsewhere before looking to Aidan for a nod of confirmation. Then he vanished into the back, only to return moments later. With only the battery.

"Sorry, we don't have the alternator in stock. But tell you what, let me see…" He started tapping on a computer keyboard in front of him. "Uh…yeah, I can get one of my Albuquerque stores to send one up tomorrow, if that's okay. Or I can put it on hold if you want to drive on down there and pick it up yourself."

"Damn," Winnie muttered, then turned to Aidan. "I can't possibly ask you to drive to Albuquerque. The round trip would take, what? Two hours, at least?"

"Probably three, this time of day." Aidan gritted his back teeth. "But I don't mind. Really."

"Of course you mind, it would mean giving up most of your day. And then I wouldn't be able to leave before late this afternoon, anyway. Call me crazy, but I'm not real big on driving through vast stretches of nothing after dark." She turned to the clerk. "Any other supply stores in town?"

"Sure thing," the very helpful clerk—clearly as spellbound as every other male in the place—said, hauling a phone book up onto the counter. "Why don't you go ahead and call around while I take care of those folks over there, then let me know what you decide, how's that?"

With a huge sigh, Winnie pulled out her cell phone and started calling. Five minutes and as many phone calls later, she gave Aidan wide, spooked eyes.

Because, for reasons known only to God, there was not a single alternator that would fit her truck within fifty miles of Santa Fe.

* * *

One more day.

That much, she could handle, Winnie told herself as they headed back to Tierra Rosa, Annabelle panting hotly in her ear. Her skin prickled with the memory of those strong arms wrapped around her, the feel of warm, solid male chest against her back, and she thought, *Okay, so it's been a long time.*

Of course, she reminded herself, Aidan had only been saving her life, it wasn't like he *wanted* to hold her or anything, so it didn't count. Her hormones snickered and said, *Oh, believe me, honey...it counts.*

Winnie hazarded a peek at his profile as they drove—the set jaw, the dour expression, the eyes focused straight ahead—and tried to figure out why in the name of all that was holy she was attracted to the man. Not in any logical kind of way, but on some very basic level that could really mess with her head if she let it.

Oh, sure, he was good-looking—if you were into the werewolf wannabe look—but that alone wasn't enough to attract her to somebody. Anymore. Yeesh, she couldn't even remember when she'd last gone stupid over a bunch of muscles and a cute smile. Not that Aidan's smile—if he had one at all—was cute, although she dimly remembered that he'd sure smiled plenty when they'd first met, trying so hard to convince her he and June would be perfect parents for her baby....

Boom!

And that, boys and girls, was the sound of the reality boulder crashing into the middle of her very wayward thoughts. Because the bizarreness of her attraction to Aidan Black notwithstanding, his being her son's adoptive father sure as heck called a screeching halt to *that* little fantasy, didn't it—?

"Yes?" Aidan said beside her, his clipped response to his

cell phone jarring her out of pointless musings. "I'm driving, Robbie, if a state trooper sees me, I'm screwed... No, Flo didn't tell me, she mustn't have known, either.... Yes, of course, I'll be right there."

He tossed the phone into a cup holder and glanced over as a host of "uh-ohs" sprang to life in the pit of Winnie's stomach. "Apparently Robbie neglected to tell anyone he had early dismissal today. Since Flo won't be back until later, I need to pick him up." He scratched his chin. "He's already been waiting for fifteen minutes." His fingers flexed on the steering wheel. "And the school's on the way back to the property. If I drop you off first, it adds another ten minutes—"

"Not a problem," Winnie said, her throat clenching much farther down than throats normally clench.

More flexing. "Are you sure?"

"Oh, for pity's sake, Aidan. I put my big-girl panties on this morning, I can deal with it, okay?"

At least, she'd do her supercalifragilistic best.

Backpack thumping, hair flying, Robbie streaked toward them the instant they nosed into the school parking lot...only to come to a complete halt when he noticed Winnie. And, presumably, Annabelle, who'd thrust her head out Winnie's open window to do her is-life-great-or-what? barking/quivering thing. Not until the kid got closer did Winnie notice the tear-tracked cheeks, his earlier upset now apparently forgotten in the combination of shock and apprehension at seeing Winnie again.

All of which he conveniently set aside long enough to hurl a *very* indignant, "How come *nobody* picked me up?" the moment he scrambled into the backseat with the dog.

"Because *nobody* knew they let you loose early today," Aidan answered mildly, steering the truck back toward the road, and Winnie focused in front of her, hearing her child, smelling his father, trying not to combust.

"There was a notice and everything! It was in my backpack!"

"And you're sure of that, are you? Because I certainly didn't see it when I went through your backpack last night. But it's all good now, right?" Aidan said, tossing Robbie a quick grin toward the back, which Winnie caught, nearly choking on her own sucked-in breath.

Oh, dear God—she'd *totally* forgotten the dimples.

While she'd been doing all this stealth breath-sucking, Annabelle had been concentrating on making it all better, as Annabelle was given to doing, and the boy's indignation/apprehension had given over to peals of laughter. *That's how kids are supposed to sound,* Winnie thought, and then Robbie said, through the giggles, "I thought you were s'posedta leave."

"My truck had other ideas, honey. So I have to try again tomorrow."

His head poked through the front seats, earning him a growled, "Robson! Seat belt!"

As he wriggled back to click his belt in place, though, he said, "Is it okay if Jacob comes over later, like around two? He said his mom said it was okay if it was okay with you." And it occurred to her that Robbie loomed much larger on her radar—for obvious reasons—than she did on his.

She saw Aidan's eyes jerk toward the rearview mirror, the shock scoot across his features. Winnie could practically hear the whirring in his head, that he'd already lost his morning, and now, with Robbie unexpectedly home from school and Florita gone, there went the afternoon, too. But he only nodded and said, "Sure. Why not?"

So much for the three-day grounding, Winnie thought, smiling, until Robbie said, "Winnie, too? Like right now, I mean, not later." She wasn't sure who stiffened more, Aidan or her.

"Um…" he said, and Robbie said, "Please?" and Winnie twisted around to say, "Oh, sugar…I don't know…I've already taken up a lot of your father's time, he probably needs to get back to work…"

"It's okay," Aidan muttered, and Winnie's eyes darted to his face, silently pleading, *Work with me here.* A tactic that only works if the other person makes eye contact with you. Which, damn it all to hell, Aidan wasn't doing.

So, because Robbie was now promising to make lunch himself if his Dad had stuff to do, Winnie sighed and thought, *What could another few hours hurt?* and said, "I'd love to," and Robbie let out a "Yes!!!" behind her that both warmed and nearly broke her heart, all at the same time.

What's going through your head? Aidan mentally directed to Winnie, as he followed her and Robbie from room to room. If nothing else, he was impressed by her ability to roll with the punches. To smile and laugh when he sincerely doubted she felt much like making merry.

He should take notes, he grumpily mused, at the same time thinking there's nothing like a surprise guest to make you see your house through fresh eyes. The kitchen was Florita's domain; beyond that, although she did her best to keep the dust bunnies from achieving world domination, she'd long since given up the good fight against the clutter.

Not that Aidan and June had been slobs, exactly, as much as obsessing about housework simply hadn't been high on their list—hence their decision to hire a house-keeper. Although the great room, and June's studio loft above it, were no longer command central for whatever causes June had been championing at the time, the space still had that air of perpetual upheaval about it, toys and magazines and June's vast folk art collection spread out helter-skelter over furnishings that seemed to go out of their way to not match.

And his unexpected guest wasn't missing a thing.

It startled Aidan to realize how much it mattered, what she thought. That she'd undoubtedly be seeking reassurance, even if only subconsciously, that she'd chosen well.

Especially when they came to Robbie's room. Would she see the overflowing bookshelves and massive dinosaur model collection and constellation-decorated ceiling as evidence that they had, indeed, given him advantages she could never have afforded…or that they'd overindulged him? That they'd kept him safe…or isolated?

Did she see Aidan's desire to spare Robbie the truth of her identity as rightly protective…or lamely suffocating?

Was she thinking, *Oh, good…I did the right thing?*

Or, Oh, God…what was I thinking?

"Dad!" Robbie said, startling him. "Do you have to follow us *everywhere?*"

The dismissal smarted out of all proportion to its intent as a red-faced Winnie muttered, "You know, honey, your daddy probably isn't comfortable with leaving you alone with me, since I'm still basically a stranger." As then her gaze swerved to Aidan's, her brows lifted as if to say, *Entirely your call, buddy.*

Then Aidan saw in his son's eyes a plea he didn't entirely understand. Or like, frankly. Because somewhere along the line, things had slipped completely out of his control…even if on some deeper, undefined level Aidan understood that the more he tried to hang on to that so-called control, the more it would elude him. June had always been the one disposed to take life as it came, to trust events to unfold as they should…the very character trait that had drawn him to her to begin with. And, perhaps, the one he'd missed the most since her death.

So he was more than a little startled to hear himself say, "Not a problem, I'll be off then to start lunch. Are grilled cheese sandwiches and soup from a tin all right? I'm not exactly a wizard in the kitchen." ·

And in *Winnie's* eyes he saw an unsettling blend of gratitude, compassion and a determination to stay strong that wrenched something loose inside him. "Soup and grilled cheese'll be just fine and dandy," she said, smiling and kind and forgiving and patient and flexible.

In other words, a right pain in the arse.

Chapter Six

It was some time after Aidan went off to tend to their meal before Winnie really tuned in to whatever Robbie was saying. Clearly, Aidan was anxious about what might happen, that maybe she'd slip up, or that Robbie might blow. Heaven knows he had nothing to worry about on the first score, despite the near-constant ache in the center of her chest. But she knew there was no way of predicting a child's reaction to a recent—or even not so recent—loss, what might set him off. Which was why there was no way she'd disrespect Aidan's wishes, whether he trusted, or believed, her or not.

One more day…

"And up there on those shelves," Robbie said, "are all the Lego sets I built. Cool, huh?"

Her gaze lifting to the high shelf that hugged the ceiling along two whole walls, Winnie nodded. "Very cool," she said, thinking, *Boy, kiddo—you really, really lucked out.*

Light poured through a pair of huge windows into a child's dream of a room, three times the size of hers at home, a cross between a video arcade, museum and library. Not that she imagined Robbie had a clue how fortunate he was, since he had nothing to compare it to. Nor, it occurred to her, would he have known what he'd been missing, if she'd—

Uh, uh, uh.

She stopped in front of an eight-by-ten photo of Robbie and his parents, taken a few years ago. Like those Russian nesting dolls, a grinning Aidan had June wrapped in his arms from behind; an even more broadly smiling June held an obviously giggling Robbie the same way. Winnie's gaze touched each one in turn, lingering a little too long on Aidan's image.

"That's my mom," Robbie said beside her, holding some sort of flying contraption built out of a gazillion interlocking plastic bits.

"I figured. How old were you?"

He shrugged. "Dunno. Like five? She wasn't sick then, I know that." He spun and sank with a bounce on his bed, the twin-size mattress covered with a wool blanket ablaze in a bold geometric pattern of bright oranges and yellows and reds. As the scent of browned butter drifted into the room from downstairs, he said, "Mom painted the stars and stuff on my ceiling all by herself."

Winnie dutifully looked up. "Wow. That must've taken her a long time."

"I guess. I was in the hospital with 'pendicitis, she had it all done by the time I got back."

A dull knife twisted in her own belly, that he'd had appendicitis and she hadn't known. That if she hadn't turned chicken, she would have. Annoyance churning around the knife, she looked over at his bookcases. "That's a lot of books. Have you read them all?"

"Some. Mom and Dad read the others to me. Mom,

mostly." He paused. "Even when she was too sick to get around very much, she still read to me."

The ache of loss in his voice brought tears to Winnie's eyes, even as it hit her what this was all about. "It feels good to talk about your mom, huh?"

Turning the plane or whatever it was over and over in his hands, Robbie finally nodded, further confirming her suspicions when he said, "Dad doesn't like it when I talk about her."

"What makes you think that?"

The boy's shoulders jerked. "I just know, that's all."

Winnie lowered herself to sit beside him. "What about Flo?" she said gently. "Or…maybe somebody at school?"

"Flo always looks like she wants to cry. And at school it's like…" On a pushed breath, he set the plane down and looked at her. "Ever since Mom died, nobody treats me normal anymore. The grown-ups all act like I'm gonna go weird on 'em or something, and the other kids…sometimes I think they're scared if they say something to me about Mom dying, it could happen to them, too. It sucks," he added on a long sigh.

"Yeah. It does." It had been a lot like that for her, too, after her own parents died. Especially the part about not being treated normally, when the one thing a child most craves is exactly that—for things to start feeling normal again, as much and as soon as possible. She hesitated, then folded her arms across her midsection. "You really should talk to your daddy about how you feel."

"I can't."

"Sure you can." She ducked her head to look into his face. "Would you like me to say something to him for you? Would that help?"

A shrug.

"But if you can talk to me—"

"That's diff'rent."

"Can you tell me why?"

Another shrug. From downstairs, Aidan called them to lunch. "Robbie," she said gently, getting to her feet. "I'm not…" She stopped, cleared her throat. "I'm not gonna be around much longer. You've gotta find somebody to talk to, okay? And maybe, now some time's passed, your dad's more ready than you think?"

"He's calling, we better go," Robbie said, tossing the plane onto the mattress and sprinting toward the door, leaving Winnie behind.

In more ways than one.

Ladling out the soup into three brightly painted bowls, Aidan glanced up when Winnie came into the kitchen. Alone.

"Where's the lad?"

"Washing up," she said, clearly avoiding his gaze.

"So…how did it go?"

"Give me a minute," she said softly, picking up the sandwich plates from the counter to set them on the plank wood table taking up most of the room, then reaching over to fiddle with the dried flower arrangement that had been there forever. On a sigh, she straightened, her hands stuffed into her sweatshirt pockets, her gaze drifting toward the patio doors and the forest beyond. "Great house."

"Is that your attempt at steering the conversation into safer waters?"

He heard a short, humorless laugh. "Right now I've got a hole the size of Montana in my chest. And I have no earthly idea how to fix it. So humor me. I say, *Great house.* And you say, *Thanks.* Or whatever, I don't care."

Even though there was no reason to feel even remotely sorry for her—after all, none of this would be happening if she'd stayed in Texas—some rusty, unused part of him did, anyway. At least enough to play along. For the moment. "I'm afraid it's a bit messy—"

"Forget it, it just looks lived in, that's all. Miss Ida'd have a hissy fit if her house wasn't spotless at all times, but all that cleaning and polishing and straightening up always seemed like a huge waste of time and energy to me. What's the point of putting things away if you're just gonna use 'em again in a few hours?"

"Exactly," Aidan said, feeling better. Over the sound of running water from the hall bath, Robbie started singing at the top of his lungs. Winnie smiled.

"He always do that?"

"He used to," Aidan said, pouring milk for Robbie, tea for them. "All the time. What he lacks in talent he makes up for in enthusiasm."

Winnie quietly laughed, then fiddled with the end of her sleeve for a moment before saying, "Um…if it'd help, I'd be glad to hang around while Robbie has his friend over. Just until Flo gets back, I mean. To free you up so you can get back to work?"

"I couldn't ask you—"

"Just to make sure the boys stay out of trouble. Believe me, they won't want some dumb girl getting in their way. So there's no ulterior motive here, I swear," she said, her cheeks pinking. "And anyway, it's the least I can do after all your help with my truck."

Aidan watched her for a moment, then said quietly, "This is the first time since June's death Robbie's asked to have a friend over, didya know?"

"Ohmigosh…no. I didn't."

"So it won't bother me to have another child in the house. Still…"

"Let me guess. June had always been the one to entertain the kids."

His cheeks warmed. "I never really know what to do with them, y'see. So actually…I'm very grateful for your offer."

"Then we're all set. And it's not like I'm trying to keep

what Robbie and I talked about a secret or anything. It's just…" She pulled back a chair from the table and plunked into it, pushing up her sleeves. "He says he can't talk to you about June."

"What?" Aidan's brows slammed together. "Of course he can talk to me!"

"Well, he doesn't think so. Kids are real sensitive, Aidan," she said gently. "If it makes you uncomfortable to talk about her, he's gonna pick up on that. I know, I know…I'm sticking my nose in where it doesn't belong," she said, looking miserable. "But it was either that or not tell you at all. And anyway, it's not a criticism, believe me."

"Isn't it?"

"Of course not. Everybody deals with grief in their own way. I clammed up, too, after my parents died. I had to work things out by myself. And my grandmother…" She huffed out another one of those mirthless laughs. "It seemed the only way Ida could deal with losing her daughter was to keep reminding herself what a disappointment she'd been."

One hand reached over to straighten out a spoon. "But Robbie's different. He needs somebody to listen to him. To share the memories. If that's too painful for you, then maybe you need to think about finding somebody—"

"Wait a minute…are you sayin' he's talking to *you* about his mother?"

After a moment, she nodded. "How's that for irony?"

"But I'm his *father,* for God's sake!"

"My point exactly," Winnie said over the sound of Robbie's sneakered feet pounding down the hall, turning to smile for the lad as he burst into the room.

The light in the studio had nearly faded beyond usefulness when Aidan heard Flo's heels *clack-clacking* behind him, followed by, "So what's up with Winnie makin' pizza in *my* kitchen with Robbie and some kid I don' know from Adam?"

"About damn time you returned," he groused, half to her, half to the painting as he wiped his brush on a rag. "And that's Jacob. Who I know you've met before, because I have."

"They all start to look the same after a while," Flo said, the clacking—and her perfume—getting closer. "The red over here," she said, flapping her hand at the right side of the painting. "It's out of whack with the rest of it."

"And you're forgettin' our agreement." Aidan detested having people around while he was working, commenting on a piece that wasn't finished yet. He had a hard enough time taking criticism after he'd wrestled the bloody things into submission—at which point it was moot, anyway— but editorial remarks while the work was in progress were absolutely verboten. Even June, who had actually let a filmmaker hang around her studio for a week—a thought that gave Aidan heartburn—had respected that Aidan did not work by committee. His housekeeper, however, had yet to evolve that far.

In fact, she shrugged and said, "An' how is it that the woman you were ready to ship to another planet yesterday is cooking your dinner and watching your kid today?"

"Her car died. I said I'd fix it but the part won't be in until tomorrow."

"An' that's reason enough to leave her alone with Robbie? You trust her that much, that fast?"

"Yes." Aidan frowned at the painting. "You really think there's too much red?"

"Are you kidding? It looks like you slaughtered a pig in here. And I don' know what you're thinking, boss, but it don' take no crystal ball to predict there's gonna be broken hearts in your future. Or did you miss the way she was looking at Robbie?"

Of course he hadn't missed it, that combination of amazement and regret that made his grilled cheese curdle in his stomach. And he *didn't* know why he trusted her, why he was willing to take that risk. But the thought had come…if she had the courage to give herself this one day, what skin was it off his nose to do the same? To share with her what she'd so generously given to him and June?

"So how's Tess?" he now said, getting up and turning his back on the painting. "Due pretty soon, isn't she?"

"Two weeks. I helped her get the baby's room set up, she was hoping maybe Rico'd get leave by now so he'd be here when the baby comes, but now it's not looking good for him to get home before sometime in the spring. Amazing, with cell phones and computers and everything, how he can call home almost anytime he wants, all the way from Iraq. Not like when my Jorge was in 'Nam, it'd be weeks, sometimes, between letters—"

"Does Robbie ever talk to you about June?"

Flo shut her open mouth. Opened it again to say, "I tried to goose him into talking about her—in the beginning, you know, even though it was hard for me, too—but he wouldn't bite. I finally figured when he wanted to talk, he would. Why?"

"Just wondering," Aidan said, staring distractedly at the painting. "Maybe you could make a salad to go with the pizza?"

"Yeah, boss," Flo said in a funny voice. "I'll go do that."

Aidan frowned after her, thinking, *What the hell…?*

There's not a woman alive, Winnie thought as she oversaw two pairs of little hands as they liberally sprinkled black olives and sliced peppers over the sauce-drenched pizza crust, who would've missed Flo's you're-encroach-ing-on-my-territory vibes. Although whether they were due to Winnie's being with Robbie or being in Flo's kitchen, she couldn't say. Probably a bit of both.

"Oh, don't do that," Winnie now said as the woman

went behind them with much sighing and eye-rolling and jewelry-jangling, scraping off cutting boards and wiping up flour and putting things back in the refrigerator. "We were gonna clean up our mess as soon as the pizza went in the oven."

"It's no bother, it's my job," Flo said, somehow managing to not look directly at her while keeping an eye on her at the same time.

Honestly.

"Is it ready?" Robbie said, radiating pride, and Winnie's heart turned over in her chest.

"It's ready."

The pizza in the oven, Winnie sent boys and dog off to play while it was baking, then grabbed a sponge to clean the one spot the housekeeper had somehow missed. "Didn't mean to step on your toes, but it was getting late and the boys were hungry—"

"And jus' what do you think you're doing?"

Winnie blinked. "Making supper?"

"Don' you play that game with me," Flo said, jabbing a long-nailed finger in Winnie's direction. "Why are you making Robbie fall for you, when you know you're only gonna leave an' break his heart?"

When Winnie found her voice again, she said, "What on earth are you talking about? I've been here exactly one afternoon! I hardly think—"

"Then maybe you should think more. Especially before you act."

Winnie folded her arms over her whumping heart. "It wasn't like I *planned* on being here today! In fact, I was all set to leave this morning, only then my stupid truck broke down, so I came up here for a freakin' phone book because there isn't one in the house and where else was I supposed to go? Only Aidan said he didn't know where it was—"

"It's right *there!*" Flo said, exasperated, pointing to

something that sure looked like a phone book, right underneath the telephone on the wall next to the fridge. "Where it's been ever since I came to work here!"

"I'm only tellin' you what he said," Winnie said, thinking, *Men, honest to God. "Anyway,"* she continued while she was on her roll, "so then he took it on himself to play mechanic, which resulted in him taking me into Santa Fe, only nobody there had the part I needed. Then we picked Robbie up from school because apparently Aidan had no idea it was a short day and you weren't around, and the kid wanted me to come to lunch and I would've backed out but *Aidan* said it was okay, okay? Not me. So once I was here I offered to watch the kids so Aidan could get some work done since he'd already lost half a day on account of that damn part, and then it got late so I went ahead and made supper because it seemed the logical thing to do. So if that makes me some kind of, I don't know, manipulative hussy or something, well, ex-cuse me for living!"

Florita looked at her for several seconds, burst out laughing, then shook her head. "I'm sorry, it's jus' that I worry 'bout them, you know? An' I see you worming your way into this family, making pizza in my kitchen, an' I think, this chick, she doesn't have any family of her own—"

"And you think I'm trying to find an instant family *here?*" When Flo shrugged, Winnie sighed, figuring this rat terrier of a housekeeper was the least of her worries. "Trust me, nothing could be further from my mind. All I was doing was *making supper.* And then tomorrow Aidan will fix my truck and I'll be outta everybody's hair for good."

Flo gave her a speculative look, then turned to the meat-locker-size refrigerator to get out salad fixings. "You made the pizza from scratch?"

If that was Flo's attempt at being conciliatory, Winnie supposed she could climb down off her high horse for a minute or two. "I found flour and yeast and that pizza stone under the cabinet, so I made up a crust dough earlier. It was either that or meat loaf for fifty."

Winnie saw the woman's glittery mouth twitch as she dumped lettuce, tomatoes and a cucumber on the counter. "You should be married."

"I'll put it on my list. But this is your business how?"

"You're in my kitchen," she said, pulling several leaves off a head of romaine, "I get to ask the questions. Besides, it's boring as hell up here, I got nothin' else to do."

Grabbing the cucumber and peeler, Winnie went to the sink to strip it. "What can I say, it just hasn't happened for me yet."

"Some *pendejo* dumped you?" she heard behind her.

"More than one, actually," Winnie said, getting the gist.

"Pretty girl like you, I'm surprised the men aren't lined up for miles."

"I live in a town smaller than this one, Flo," Winnie said, thinking, *Pretty?* "There's not enough available men to line up for twenty feet, let alone miles. And half of those…" She shuddered.

"So you should move."

"Don't think I haven't considered it. But I couldn't before now. And anyway, it's not that easy to pull up roots that deep. Especially when you haven't had two seconds to think about what comes next." Winnie handed the now naked cucumber to Flo, then glanced outside just as the last rays of sunset gilded the landscape. "It's really beautiful up here. Closest thing we've got to mountains back home is the occasional dead armadillo by the side of the road."

"The winters can be a bitch, though."

"Can't be any worse than gettin' a sand facial every time you walk out your door."

Flo almost chuckled. "Tierra Rosa's jus' like any other small town, it's got its good and its bad."

"You're still here."

"Like you said…deep roots."

Winnie slid up onto a stool across from Flo, propping one booted foot on the railing at the base of the breakfast bar, her arms crossed. "I gather June was from around here, too?"

A shadow crossed the housekeeper's features before she said, "Nearby. Next town over. Her folks're gone now, too." Her knife passing through a tomato in slow motion, she added, "Sometimes, I can almos' still feel her presence."

"Whose presence? June's?"

"Yes. Especially as it gets closer to *Los Días de Los Muertos*. You know about that?"

"The Days of the Dead? Sure. Well, a little. A couple Mexican families back home observe it. I never really got it, myself."

"You think it's spooky, no?" Flo said with a grin. "But it's not like that for us, it's a celebration. We don't go all out the way they do in Mexico, maybe, but it's still important. We get together, we remember those who've gone on before, we laugh, we tell stories, we show them we haven't forgotten them, that they still live in our memories. Our hearts. So in a way, they really do 'come back' to visit us, you see? It's a time to show we're not afraid of death, because it can't really take our loved ones from us. Not in the way that most matters."

"Oh. When you put it that way, it makes a lot of sense. But what if…?"

Flo's eyes lifted to hers. "What?"

"Nothing," Winnie said, refusing to let moroseness gain a foothold. Like wondering about people who die with no family. Who celebrates their lives? Who remembers them?

"You know," Flo was saying, "everybody loved Miss June. She could cut a person down to size with three words if they had it coming, but *Dios mío*, I never knew anyone with a bigger heart." Her mouth thinned. "I know people sometimes said things. Mean things. Because Miss June was so much older than the boss. But what does love know about age?" she added with a shrug. "About *friendship*. 'Cause you never saw two people who were better friends. And I know he still misses her real bad."

"I'm sure he does," Winnie said, thinking, *Okay, cutie, time for a reality check.* That she was leaving the following day. That she was smart enough not to confuse chemistry and sympathy and loneliness with anything real. "You call him 'the boss'?"

Flo smiled. "Miss June would call him that sometimes, just to get a rise out of him. They'd be arguin' about somethin', an' she get this real amused look on her face, and go 'Whatever you say, b-boss…'"

The last words were barely out of the housekeeper's mouth before she dissolved into embarrassed tears. Winnie immediately went to her and wrapped her in her arms, getting the strangest, strongest feeling that if June had any idea how mopey everybody was around here, she'd be hugely pissed.

And that while Winnie was here, maybe she should see what she could do about that.

Chapter Seven

Winnie Porter was a strange bird indeed, Aidan decided as he sat across from her at the dining table, its dings and gouges probably hailing from New Mexico's territorial days.

He'd hung outside the kitchen, listening to her and Flo's conversation probably far longer than was politic, simply because he'd been too mesmerized to do anything else. Her moods apparently dipped and swerved like a roller coaster, with every bit of the accompanying dizziness and nausea. Women were hard enough to understand when they were levelheaded; one like Winnie...

"Why was six afraid of seven?" Robbie piped up, his mouth full of fresh, aromatic, bubbly-cheesed pizza.

"I have no idea," Winnie said, aiming a wink in Aidan's direction, and he thought, *What?* "Why was six afraid of seven?"

"Because *seven ate nine!*" Robbie said, both he and Jacob, exploding into knee-slapping laughter, which got

Annabelle to barking and spinning in circles for no apparent reason. Winnie laughed, too, just as hard, even though Aidan sincerely doubted she'd never heard the joke before. Then she launched into a series of truly terrible riddles, half of which the boys already knew—which only seemed to make them laugh harder—and the laughter and the barking crescendoed until it seemed the very room would burst.

Winnie's eyes touched his, begging him to join in.

Barely able to breathe, Aidan got up from the table to refill his tea glass, at which point he realized the jollity had apparently infected his housekeeper, as well. *Now this is more like it,* he thought he heard her say, although it didn't really sound like her voice, it sounded like—

He shook his head to clear it. He was knackered, was all, having not slept well in months. Which probably accounted for why the room suddenly seemed brighter than he remembered, the reds and golds and rich blues vibrant in the warm overhead light. He squinted at the fixture: Had Flo changed the bulbs to a higher wattage?

His glass refilled, Aidan returned to his seat. Winnie looked up, grinning full out, breathless, her cheeks flushed, and *Thank God you're leaving* and *Too bad you're leaving* collided underneath his skull like a pair of daft footballers.

"Dad! Dad! Guess what Winnie taught us?"

"Three-card monte?" Aidan said drily, and Robbie said, "Huh?" as Winnie said, "Honestly, Aidan, give me *some* credit," and Robbie said, "No—chess!"

Aidan looked at Winnie. "Chess?"

"Yeah, he had that beautiful set on the shelf in his room, I asked him if he knew how to play and he said no, so I taught him. Him and Jacob," she said with the kind of smile for Robbie's friend that young boys had been falling in love with since God did that little hocus-pocus thing with Adam's rib.

Aidan swallowed down the flare of annoyance, that June had ordered the Harry Potter set for Robbie for his eighth birthday with explicit instructions that Aidan teach their son how to play. That Winnie knew how to play chess.

Not to mention everyone who crossed her path.

Except Aidan, of course. Aidan was immune to being played—

"It's so cool," Robbie said. "Almost as cool as Mario Galaxy— Hey!" he squawked as a bit of black olive bounced off his nose. "Who did that?"

"Who did what?" Winnie said, all innocence as she took a sip of her iced tea, and Aidan opened his mouth, only to close it again, refusing to let himself feel…

Alive?

"*Somebody* threw an olive at me!"

"It was you!" Jacob yelled, eyes alight, pointing at Winnie. "I saw you!"

"Was not," Winnie said, picking a pepperoni slice off her pizza and chucking it at Jacob, which set off a whole new round of giggles. Then a mushroom bounced off Aidan's forehead and the boys roared, and from the other end of the kitchen Flo threw her hands up and muttered something in Spanish that Aidan only half heard, and when he met Winnie's gaze she cocked her head at him, grinning, her eyes full of mischief and mayhem, and he thought, *No.*

But not before the sucker punch hit. With far more devastation than the mushroom. Because from somewhere deep, deep inside him, a funny, fuzzy feeling bubbled up, like inhaling helium.

Go with it, babe…

Aidan picked up the artillerized fungus. "Lose something?" he said, his gaze locked with hers.

She grinned, full of herself. Smug. Dangerous. "Consider it a gift," she said.

Only to shriek with laughter when he threw it back.

* * *

An hour later, Aidan sneaked a glance at Winnie's face as his truck jostled down the mountain to take Winnie and Annabelle back to the Old House, then Jacob home. Behind him, the boys squealed every time the truck hit a bump. Beside him, Winnie smiled, thinking more secret Winnie thoughts. Aidan jerked his head back around, telling himself he wasn't interested. In her thoughts, or…anything else.

Now there's a lie for you.

Feeling his nostrils flare, a certain swift, hot kick to his groin, Aidan shifted gears as they navigated a particularly steep part of the road. Two years ago he wouldn't have believed it possible that the time would come when he wouldn't miss sex. Until June got sick, and things changed, and Aidan basically put his libido in cold storage.

Then June died, and what would have been the point in taking it back out?

Not that he didn't occasionally still think about That Side of Things, as his mother would say. But not so much about having sex—or not—as how strangely easy it had been to simply disconnect one or two crucial wires. That he hadn't felt deprived so much as disinterested.

Until tonight.

Which was making him confused as all hell. Not to mention cranky. Crank*ier.*

The truck bumped up in front of the Old House; when Winnie opened the door, Aidan told the boys to sit tight, he'd be back straightaway, and got out before he caught Winnie's look. Because he knew there'd be a Look.

Sure enough, as soon as they were out of earshot her eyes slid to his. "Walkin' me to the door's kinda overkill, don't you think?"

"I'm just setting a good example for the lads."

"Ah." She pulled the persimmon-colored jacket closed, shivering; nightfall had sucked all the warmth out of the air. At least, that provided by the sun.

"I just…wanted to thank you for watching the boys. And for the pizza, it was great."

"You're welcome—"

"And for gettin' Robbie out of himself like that."

Her grin was cautious. "Yeah, nothin' like a good food fight to shake things up. Although Flo may never speak to any of us again."

Aidan smiled back, telling himself that her lips were just lips. That this was a helluva time for That Side of Things to kick in again. "She'll survive. Besides, the dog cleaned most of it up already."

"Good old Annabelle," Winnie said warmly to the beast, who barked up at her. Then burped.

"It should've been me, though," he said.

"To lick the food off the floor?"

"No," he said on a half laugh, then sighed, raking one hand through his hair. Which really was getting too long. "To teach Robbie how to play chess." He paused. "To make him laugh again."

He caught her gaze dipping from his hair to someplace below his neck. "I didn't mean to step on any toes, honest—"

"And I didn't mean to imply you had. Well, not too much anyway. What I mean to say is, what's important is seeing Robbie happy. How that came about is immaterial." Tamping down the tremor of disloyalty, he said, "I think June would be pleased."

Her eyes lifted, glittering in the half-assed porch light. She nodded, then turned to unlock the door. "So. What time should I be ready tomorrow?"

"So you're really going, then?"

Winnie twisted around, at least as shocked as he. Then

she sighed. "I had a blast today, Aidan. I really did. But it wasn't easy."

"No, I don't suppose it was," he said, appalled to discover how badly he wanted to hold her. To rub her back and tell her it would be okay. "Well, then. Is eight too early?"

"No, eight's fine—"

"I'm going t'do better, Winnie. With Robbie, I mean. Whatever's still goin' on inside *my* head, Robbie's only a child. And I know he needs to be getting on with things. With bein' a boy, enjoying life. If y'know what I mean."

After a moment, she crossed her arms, shivering slightly, her eyes soft with concern. "This is only a suggestion, okay? But Flo was talkin' about the Day of the Dead, about how it's not morbid at all, but instead a way to celebrate those who've gone on. So maybe, I don't know…you should think about you and Robbie holding some kind of vigil for June? Because maybe remembering will help ease the pain? Because…because if I were her, I sure as heck wouldn't be happy knowing that you and Robbie weren't."

A sudden gust of woodsmoke-laced air made Aidan's eyes burn, a shiver lick at his spine, even as those guileless eyes did their best to melt something long frozen inside him. "Y'might be on to something at that," he said with a jerk of his head, then added, "It's dipping into the t'irties tonight, are you sure you've got enough firewood?"

Winnie's mouth pulled into a small, damnably understanding smile. "Plenty, thanks. So…see you tomorrow," she said, slipping inside the house and shutting the door before he could make any more of a fool of himself than he already had.

Dad's footsteps were so soft outside Robbie's room he barely got his thumb out of his mouth in time. He knew he was way too old to be still sucking his thumb, but sometimes it made him feel less jumpy inside—

"Laddie?" Dad whispered, right by his bed. Robbie rolled; in the dark, Dad was a big blob, the light from the hallway making this weird glow all around him. "Ah. So you're not asleep."

Robbie shook his head, and Dad sat on the edge of his bed, making Robbie tumble toward him. They both laughed, a little. Then Dad leaned over him with his hands on either side of Robbie's shoulders, making him feel safe. Now he could see his face, even if his hair hung down in his eyes. He was smiling. Sorta.

"Y'had a good time tonight, didn't'ya?"

Robbie nodded. "It was…"

"What?"

"It kinda reminded me of before. With Mom."

"I know. It did me, too."

"Winnie's really funny, huh?"

"That she is," Dad said in a strange voice, then pushed Robbie's hair out of his face. "I'd forgotten how good it felt to laugh. To be a little crazy."

A little crazy? Before Mom got sick—even after, until she got really bad—Dad and Mom used to go *nuts*, cracking each other up all the time. Robbie remembered sometimes laughing so hard his stomach would hurt. Tonight was the closest he'd come to feeling like that in a really long time.

Dad's mouth got all twisted. "It's been hard on both of us, this last year," he said, and Robbie nodded, not sure what he was supposed to say. But Dad wasn't finished. "It occurs to me that maybe I've fallen down on the job in my duties as a father. It wasn't something I did on purpose, I just…" He let out a big breath. "I just want you to know, you can talk to me. About…anything a'tall."

"About Mom, you mean."

"Yes," he said, smiling a little. "About Mom."

Robbie frowned. "I didn't think you even thought about her all that much."

"Oh, Robbie," Dad said on another breath, this one even longer, "I think about your mother all the time. But it's been hard for me to talk about her because it hurts so much. Do y'see?"

"Yeah, I guess."

"But that doesn't mean *you* can't talk about her. To me, I mean. To be honest, I don't think Mom would be very happy about the way I've been acting since she died."

In the dark, Robbie felt his eyes open wide. He couldn't remember Dad ever coming right out and saying that Mom had *died*. In a way, he felt like this big rock had rolled off his chest…only to get stuck in his throat. Part of him wanted to tell Dad everything, about how he sometimes felt like Mom was in the Old House, about how he missed the way Mom would sing, really badly and so loud birds would fly up out of the trees. About how he remembered the time she burned the stew she was trying to make and the whole house got full of smoke and how much he missed the way they used to laugh all the time.

But he couldn't get the words past that dumb rock.

In the dark, he saw Dad's eyes go all shiny. Then he nudged Robbie over so he could lie down beside him, holding him against his chest.

"It's okay if you're not ready, laddie," Dad whispered into his hair. "But whenever you are, I'm right here, I promise." He kissed Robbie's forehead. "How's that?"

His eyes watery, all Robbie could do was nod.

The next morning, Winnie came out of the bathroom to find Annabelle whining in great excitement at the bottom of the front door, followed by the muffled sounds of somebody messing about with tools and such out front. Momentarily forgetting she was only wearing Ida's ratty old chenille robe, she swung open the door to an arctic blast that swirled inside like a cat looking for someplace warm.

Madly toweling her hair before it froze, she called out, "It's not even eight yet, so don't tell me I'm late!" Then she frowned. "What are you doing?"

From underneath the hood of her truck, Aidan mumbled something about going into town early for the part, there'd been no need for her to go, too, before he popped into view, slamming shut the hood. He was all woodsy today, in a checkered jacket and cute little beanie pulled down over his waves, which she realized—too late—only made his jaw look even sharper and his mouth even more...eye-catching. "I'm just now done, actually. So you can be on your way anytime you like, the truck's ready to go."

Okay, by rights she should be leaping about with great joy, hallelujah, praise the Lord. Instead she squeaked out, "Really?"

Aidan frowned at her. She was finally beginning to understand that frowning was his normal expression, not to take it personally. "I t'ought you'd be pleased. Because this way you'll be home before dark?"

Suddenly aware assorted important bits on her person were about to flash freeze, Winnie held up one finger and ducked inside to yank on some ten-odd layers of clothes, all the while reminding herself that if her reaction to Aidan last night as he stood there, looking contrite as hell and far sexier than was good for either of them, was any indication, she should be down on her knees in gratitude. Especially as those assorted important bits began to defrost and remind her—rudely—exactly how much time had passed since they'd been put to good use. Or any use a'tall, as he might say.

As she tugged on her boots, she idly wondered if she should be questioning her sanity. Then she comforted herself with the thought that she only had to hang on for a little while longer, and she'd be out of there with her dignity intact. Along with her heart and those assorted other bits.

Because, yes, leaving Robbie was going to be a bitch and a half, but the sooner she did, the better. Leaving his father, however, she thought as she scrubbed at her hair one last time with the dry side of the towel, wasn't supposed to cause so much as a twinge of regret. A flutter of disappointment. A prickle of…whatever the hell was prickling.

Hoping her hair still-damp wouldn't turn into icicles, she went back outside, where Aidan was talking into his cell. Frowning, of course.

"That was Flo," he said, clapping the cell phone shut and striding back toward his own truck, all concentration of purpose. "It was half in Spanish, but the upshot was that Tess went into labor, Flo ran out to her car, remembered she was supposed to take Robbie to school, tried to get to her phone in her purse to call me and between not paying attention and the chickens and those stupid high heels she wears, she stumbled. And fell. And now she can't bend her wrist."

"Oh, no—!"

But Aidan had shifted into Man Take Action mode. "I suppose I'll go back to the house and pick her and Robbie up," he muttered as he yanked open his truck door, "drop Robbie off at school, then go get Tess and take them to the hospital—"

"Aidan!"

He stopped mid-sentence, giving Winnie a look that might have been almost comical if the situation hadn't been so serious. And she could have said something like, *Give everybody my love, then,* or *What a shame I can't stick around and help out,* but of course she couldn't do that—

"What?" he said.

She cast a brief, longing glance at her truck, telling herself it couldn't actually look crestfallen that, for the second time in as many days, plans had changed. On a heartfelt sigh, she returned her gaze to Aidan.

"I know you think you're 'The Man,' but not even you can take three people to three different places at one time."

A muscle popped in his jaw. "Robbie's school's on the way to the hospital and both women'll be going there—"

"And last time I checked hospitals didn't generally fix wrists in the maternity wing. Besides, who's got Miguel?"

"Ah, hell, I forgot about him—"

"So I noticed." She held out her hand. "Give me my keys. I'll pick up Robbie and Flo, you go ahead and get Tess and Miguel, and we'll meet up in Maternity. I know where the hospital is," she said to his frown, "I passed it when I was out driving the other day."

"But what about getting back to Texas?"

"I imagine it'll still be there tomorrow," she said, trudging back to her truck.

Naturally, Robbie was none too pleased to be shut out of all the excitement. And Winnie pitied his teacher, that was for sure. But the situation was already perilously close to one of those old-time farces with people popping in and out of doors every two seconds; fielding a nine-year-old's barrage of questions on top of it was the last thing any of them needed.

She'd watched in admiration—and okay, surprise—as Aidan efficiently, and gently, wrapped the borderline hysterical Flo's rapidly swelling wrist in an elastic bandage before taking off to fetch Tess and Miguel. Now, Robbie delivered to school and Flo to the E.R.—where she'd apparently known the nurse in charge since God was a pup— Winnie hauled ass back up to maternity.

She heard his voice before she saw him, low and soothing as he apparently talked Tess through a contraction, one arm around her shoulders while the four-year-old watched, more curious than concerned. Honest to Pete…to look at the man, you'd think he coached women through labor on a regular basis.

"Done?" he asked, just brimming with fake cheer, when Tess took a deep breath. Only after she nodded, though, did Aidan look up and notice Winnie. And there it was, the *thank* God *we made it to the hospital in time* look in his eyes. But on the surface? Mr. Cool.

Snort.

"Good, you're here," he said. "If you don't mind getting her checked in, I'll just run down and see how Flo's doing. Did she mention her morbid fear of hospitals?"

"Not in so many words, no," Winnie said, thinking of the ride with the white-lipped, uncharacteristically silent, rigid-as-death Flo beside her. Not a big fan of hospitals herself, Winnie certainly hadn't needed the woman to verbalize her fear to pick up on it. "You go on, we'll be fine."

Aidan looked at her for a long moment, and Winnie gave him her *What?* look back before he quickly squeezed her shoulder and left. Winnie wasn't even aware she was ogling him as he strode off until she heard Tess say, with a short laugh, "I know what you mean."

Winnie swung her head around, wondering if the labor hormones had shorted out her brain. "Excuse me?"

"Okay, maybe the dude's a little on the weird side. But I'd stare at his backside, too. If I wasn't, you know, having a baby."

"Not to mention married?"

The immaculately coifed woman batted one immaculately manicured hand, both at odds with the stained, denim tent on her body. "A little window-shopping now and then doesn't mean you're gonna actually buy anything, if you get my drift," she said, and Winnie was suddenly hit with a weird reaction to Tess's calling Aidan weird. Even if he was. But Tess was saying to Miguel, "You remember the lady we met at the house the other day, honey?"

Puppy-dog eyes peered up at Winnie from a round face smushed into his mother's hip. "You got a dog, huh?"

Who was undoubtedly lying by the front door of the

little house, dejected at being left alone. Either that or
asleep, herding sheep.

"I sure do, sweetie—"

"Oh, *man*—"

Long French-manicured fingernails impaling Winnie's
hand, Tess's face contorted as she panted through the next
contraction—

"Mama! You peed all over!"

"Damn," Tess muttered as Winnie thought, *Cleanup in
aisle four,* signaling to the nurse's station that they could
use some help, here. As a cute little thing in Care Bear
scrubs scurried over, Miguel turned frightened eyes to
Winnie.

"Is Mama okay?"

"Yeah, dude," Tess said, beginning the long, soggy
waddle to the nurse's station. "I'm fine. It just means your
little sister's anxious to get here."

While Tess checked in—through another contraction,
insisting, "I'm fine, I'm fine" all the way—Winnie squatted
in front of the worried little boy. "Having a baby's real hard
work. But your mommy's body knows what to do, okay?
Just like it did when you came out."

Just like hers had, nine years ago, she realized as the
downside to this little Good Samaritan impulse of hers
whapped her upside the head. Damn. Then some kind soul
brought a wheelchair to take Tess to her room, and Tess
was asking Winnie to stay with her, and she thought, *You
have got to be kidding me.*

"But we barely know each other!"

"Since my aunt's kinda out of commission, it's either
you or Aidan. And if a person I don't know all that well is
gonna be looking at my hoohah, I'd rather it be somebody
with one of her own."

"Good point," Winnie said, following the wheel-
chaired preggo down the hall, holding on to Miguel's

hand, musing as how she could've been halfway to Tu-cumcari by now.

Next time, she thought, she was coming back without a conscience.

"And if that's not a sign you're supposed to be there," Elektra said in her ear some hours later, "I don't know what is."

"It's not a *sign,* E," Winnie said, slouched in a waiting room chair with Miguel curled against her, asleep. Aidan had gone to pick up Robbie from school, while, in a room down the hall, Florita—high as a kite on pain meds, her badly sprained wrist ice-packed—cheerfully coached her niece through the last stages of her labor. "It's a comedy of errors, is what it is."

Combing her fingers through the little boy's thick, dark curls, she added, "But it's nuts, you know?" At the far end of the hall, the door to the maternity wing swung open; she looked up just as Aidan and Robbie walked through, the little boy a clone of his father in his own checkered jacket and black knit cap, his gait the same loping swagger. Even as her throat jammed up, she had to smile. "I mean, if I hadn't've been here, what would they have done?"

"And you know there is no point whatsoever in thinking about the 'what ifs'," E said. "The fact is, you *were* there, and this is how things played out. It's destiny, child, and don't tell me it isn't. First your truck breaks down and then this baby coming…what else could it be?"

"Really rotten luck?"

"Ain't no such thing. Luck is about chance. Destiny's about what's *supposed* to happen." Winnie decided against arguing semantics, a lost cause with Elektra, anyway. "Somebody is sure trying to tell you you're not supposed to leave. Leastwise not yet. Not until you've fulfilled the reason why you're there."

"Which is?"

"How the hell do I know? If I had me one of them crystal balls, don't you think I'd use it to pick the right numbers to win the lottery?" Not that E had a gambling problem, but nothing short of an earthquake kept her from buying her weekly Pick 5 ticket. "And don't you go rolling your pretty blue eyes at me," she said as Winnie did just that. "*And* don't you dare ask me how things are going here, either. They're fine, same as they were yesterday, same as they'll be tomorrow and the day after that, I suspect. Oh, we got customers, I'll catch you later, baby…."

Aidan dropped into the seat beside Winnie just as she slipped her phone back into her pocket. While Robbie made a beeline for the battered blocks and cars and what-all in the play area across the room, Aidan leaned over to check on Miguel. Setting his damn pheromones loose in her personal space.

"Any news?" he said, straightening. Leaving his phero-mones littered all over creation.

"No," she said, mentally giving them the evil eye. "Flo hasn't been out to give me an update in a while. I'm thinking pretty soon, though. Or maybe that's just hope. For Tess's sake, especially."

Silence settled between them like a heavy fog. Winnie wondered if Aidan's thoughts had taken the same course as hers, back to the day Robbie was born. He and June had both been in the room. June, in fact, had cut the umbilical cord, been the first one to hold the baby. But even through the fog of adrenaline and pain and then, mercifully, the epidural, Winnie had been acutely aware of the intimacy of the moment. That the people in that room had shared a bond that neither time nor space could ever completely dissolve.

And if that didn't sound like something straight out of a Lifetime Movie Network flick…

His jacket ditched, Aidan stretched out his legs and

folded his hands on his stomach, frowning in Robbie's direction. "I was just remembering the day he was born," he said, much too softly for Robbie to hear. Still staring straight ahead, he added, "I don't think I ever said thank you."

Winnie's eyes burned. "Of course you did. June—"

"I know June did. I'm talking about m'self." He picked up a discarded newspaper from the seat next to him, glanced at it, then tossed it aside again. "I can't imagine how hard that must've been for you."

After a moment, she said, just as softly, "Thank *you*. But I didn't regret my decision."

"Not even in hindsight?"

Winnie stroked little Miguel's curls again. "I knew—still know—that I couldn't have hacked single motherhood. Not then—"

"She's here!" Flo cried from down the hall, tromping toward them in those high-heeled boots, her Ace bandage the same color blue as the gown flapping around her jeans. "Seven pounds, two ounces!" Still obviously floating from the combination of the event and certain controlled substances, the housekeeper crouched in front of Tess's little boy, waking him up. "Wanna come see your new baby sister?"

"The baby's not in Mama anymore?" the tyke said, sitting up and scrubbing one eye.

Flo laughed. "No, she's out where we can see her, an' she's *beautiful*, and Mama's fine, an' she's asking for her Micky, she wants you to meet the baby!" She stood, holding out her good hand. "So let's go!"

Yawning, the child slid off the seat and took his great-aunt's hand. "You, too!" Flo said to Winnie and Aidan and Robbie, and Winnie's stomach kicked.

"Oh, no, I don't think so," she said, getting to her feet, her hands stuffed in her jacket's pockets. "I don't even know Tess, really—"

"Are you kidding?" Flo said. "After this morning, you're family now!"

Winnie nearly jumped out of her skin when Aidan touched the small of her back, then said under his breath, "Trust me, you'll insult them if you don't go in."

So she did, even though self-preservation screamed like a banshee inside of her. *It's not about you, babycakes,* she told herself as she stepped inside the room, hanging back while the two boys eyeballed the tiny infant in Tess's arms, with her scrunched-up face and cap of matted black hair. Sure, Winnie'd seen other newborns since Robbie's birth, her girlfriends' babies, mostly. And the pang had always been there to some degree. But never like this. Between seeing the look of rapture on Tess's face as she spoke with her husband in Iraq and Robbie's being there and *Aidan's* being there and the memories…this was about as close to unbearable as it got.

But she soldiered through the next few minutes same as always, with a bright smile and the expected exclamations over the baby and an absolute refusal to feel sorry for herself. At least until she could slip out of the room unnoticed, holding in the tears until she reached the thankfully empty ladies' room.

Then, her face washed, makeup redone, hair fixed, she'd taken a deep breath and gone back into that room with her head held high and a song in her heart, even if it was sounding slightly off-key. Told herself she only imagined Aidan's frown. But then, Winnie was Queen of Ignoring Things She Didn't Want to Deal With.

Until they were leaving and Aidan took her aside, looking torn as only a very private man whose peace had just been shattered all to hell could look.

Chapter Eight

The moment Winnie disappeared, Aidan had known something was wrong. Then she returned fifteen minutes later looking a bit like a recently repaired doll, her cheeks a trifle too pink, her smile a little too bright, and he'd thought, wearily, *And just who d'you think you're fooling?*

A question he'd asked himself more than once over the past several hours.

"Lookit," he said in a low voice as Flo and the boys went on ahead, "now we're over the initial crisis, I'm sure we can manage on our own. That is, y'know, if you need to get on your way. I'd completely understand."

Naturally, Winnie looked at him as though he'd just lost what little mind he had left. And with good reason. In a weak moment, and since Flo wasn't going to be much good to anybody until her wrist got better, Aidan had already offered to move mother and baby and child to his house until she felt comfortable handling things on her own. Only then hadn't Flo immediately asked Winnie if she wouldn't mind helping out, just for a day or so? Put the poor woman in a right spot, she had.

So the least Aidan could do was let her out of it.

After a moment, Winnie snorted a little laugh. "In other words, you just remembered you want me gone as badly as I want to go. Except somehow," she added before he could fully analyze why her words agitated him so much, "I'm not seeing you juggling two kids, a newborn and at least one woman who's probably going to need assistance of a very intimate nature." Her mouth screwed up. "Maybe two."

Ah, yes. There was that. Grimacing, Aidan scrubbed a palm over his scratchy jaw. "That's a lot to ask of you—"

"After what I went through with Miss Ida? This will be a walk in the park."

Having been June's primary caregiver during the final weeks of her illness, as well, Aidan felt a wave of empathy. Winnie apparently misread his expression for something else. "Look," she said on a sigh, continuing down the hall after the others, "if you really don't want me to stick around, just say so—"

"I don't," he said, falling in step beside her. "But more for your sake than mine."

"I told you, I've got no problem with taking care—"

"I'm not talking about that." He grabbed her arm again to make her look at him. "D'you think no one noticed when you disappeared earlier? Being around Tess and the baby is obviously upsetting for you."

After another several moments of what he'd already learned to identify as the Winnie Glare, she pulled out of his grasp to bang open the door leading from the maternity wing. "And a gentleman would've kept his observations to himself," she muttered as Aidan caught the door before it smacked him in the face.

"For one thing," he huffed to her back, "I've never pretended to be a gentleman. And for another, if you're going to fall apart on me—"

"Oh, for pity's sake—!" She wheeled on him so fast he nearly crashed into her. "So I had a moment! I'm fine now. Don't go readin' more into it than it was!"

"And don't *you* go acting as though I'm deaf, blind and dumb to boot!" Aidan lobbed back. "You don't have to pretend everything's fine all the time, Winnie! Especially not around me!"

She breathed hard for a moment. "Fine, so maybe a part of me would like nothin' better than to get in my truck, go get my dog and hit the road like I'd planned. But if I've learned nothing else over the years, it's that we don't always get to choose what lands on our plates. What we *can* choose, however, is what we do with those opportunities. And sometimes that means putting our druthers aside to do what's best for somebody else. Generally speaking, I don't have a problem with that." She angled her head, the look in her eyes fierce. And uncannily familiar. "Do you—?"

"Dad?"

Aidan jerked his head around to see Robbie at the end of the hall, shifting from foot to foot as though the floor was searing his feet through the soles of his skate shoes. "What's taking you guys so long?"

"Be right there," he said, then looked back at Winnie. "If there was anybody else I could ask—"

"Well, there isn't, is there? So maybe you should be grateful I happened along when I did, or you'd be in one holy mess right now."

And there it was, that determined expression he'd been looking at for nine years, in another face. "We better get going," he muttered, starting off after his son, thinking he couldn't possibly be in any more of a holy mess than he already was.

* * *

"It's a bit dusty up here, I'm afraid," Aidan said, a half-dozen steps behind Winnie on the spiral staircase leading up to the loft. June's workspace, he'd already told her. "But I suppose you'll be comfortable enough. For a few days, anyway."

"I'm sure it'll be fine."

Actually, she decided as she looked around the cluttered, cozy space, there was something very appealing about being tucked away up here, out of sight, while still being able to see out over the kitchen and great room with its funky collection of carved *santos,* June's vibrant weavings hanging on the walls. Like a bird in its nest, she thought, feeling yet another connection with the woman who'd been her son's mother.

Despite the angled ceiling, there was plenty of room for a loom, an industrial-grade Pfaff sewing machine and cutting table, a futon layered with quilts, and all manner of shelves stuffed with vibrant yarns and fabrics. At the moment, molten light streamed in through a large, western-facing window, as if seeking the person who once called the space hers even as it tenderly caressed the abandoned equipment.

Behind her, she could feel Aidan's tension, like they were a couple of kids nosing around someplace they had no business being. "You haven't been up here since June died, have you?" she said quietly, itching to finger the beautiful quilts, afraid to touch anything for fear he'd come unglued.

"Since some months before that, actually. Flo's been after me for ages to sell the equipment, donate the yarn and such to her church's women's shelter."

"Would you ever use any of it?"

He almost laughed. "Me? No."

"Then you should seriously consider her suggestion," Winnie said, finally turning to see him looking at her in a way that makes a woman think, *Oh, yeah?* Startled, she tossed a smile in his direction, then walked over to the window to drag a finger down the dusty pane. "You know, this might make a fun game room or something for Robbie one day."

"It would that," Adam said after a long pause. From downstairs, they heard the boys yelling to each other, Flo's yelling at them in turn to keep it down, Annabelle's joyful barking about all of it. Two boys might not a herd make, but compared with a bunch of fractious chickens it was heaven. Leaning on the four-foot-high privacy wall, Aidan surveyed the living area. "I'm not sure who's more excited about Miguel's staying here, he or Robbie."

"Yet another example of how blessings can come out of adversity."

Another long pause preceded, "You really believe that claptrap, don't you?"

Winnie sat on the edge of the futon, testing it. "What I don't believe," she said, bouncing a little, "is that putting a positive spin on things is claptrap."

"Then what is it?"

When after a moment Winnie met Aidan's gaze, she saw, not the grouch, but a troubled, lonely man looking for answers. Even if he hadn't admitted to himself that's what he was doing. And her heart twanged for him, because she knew what he was feeling.

"Many's the time over the last little while when it would've been real easy to give up hope," she said. "To think there'd never be another reason to feel good about anything again. After my parents died, there wasn't a sadder little girl in the world, believe me. Then to find myself living with somebody who not only clearly found me a burden, but wouldn't allow me to grieve…"

She shook her head. "Now *that's* hell. At least it is to a ten-year-old. But you know what? I made new friends, I found family in the diner, I lucked out and got the kind of teacher who made me think maybe that's what I wanted to do, someday. But most important…I discovered I was a lot stronger than I thought I was. And thank God for that, is all I have to say. Considering the untold times I've had to put that discovery to good use since then. If you think about it, the harder you hit rock bottom, the higher you bounce, right?"

Aidan almost smiled. "If you're made of rubber, maybe."

"Well, then, I guess I am. There's good to be found in almost any situation, if you know where to look. If you're open to seeing it. It's like the old hymn—'Weeping may endure for a night, but joy cometh in the morning.'"

"And if morning never comes?"

She stood, torn between wanting to hug him and wanting to smack him. "Morning always comes, Aidan. But if you don't get your butt outta bed and go open the blinds, you'll never know, will you?"

He glared at her for another several seconds, muttered something about getting her some linens, then left.

Aidan awoke sometime in the middle of the night, vaguely aware of a dull, silvery flickering at the edge of his vision. The scent of popcorn. And what sounded like somebody unsuccessfully trying to muzzle her laughter.

He snatched his robe off the footboard, tugging it on over his T-shirt and sleep pants as he shoved his feet into his slippers, then made his way down the hall and to the middle of the stairs. From there he could see her, nearly lost inside one of June's quilts, curled up on one end of the sofa watching TV and stuffing handful after handful of popcorn into her mouth.

His mouth watered.

"What are you doing?" he asked when he reached the bottom, sending his houseguest, her sleeping dog and the popcorn flying.

"Having a heart attack," Winnie said, untangling herself

from the quilt to madly pluck scattered popcorn kernels off the hundred-year-old Navajo rug. Those the dog—now fully awake and on the case—didn't get to first, that is. Her eyes flashed silver in the light from the TV. "You're like a damn *cat,* sneaking around like that."

"I wasn't sneaking. And you haven't answered my question."

"I couldn't sleep. There's a tree or something scraping the outside wall right by the futon, it was giving me the creeps. Which is weird because usually I can sleep through anything. So I came downstairs and raided your DVD collection." The popcorn collected and dumped back in the bowl, she scootched back onto the sofa, recocooning herself in the quilt. "Although when I went to load *Duck Soup* into the player, *Monty Python and the Holy Grail* was already in it." One hand poked out of the cocoon to give him a thumb's up.

Aidan started. "Are you sure?"

"Uh, yeah. Why?"

"Because…" Because June had been the last one to watch the Monty Python movie, more than a year ago. Because he'd removed the disc himself, months later, to watch some eejit talking-animal movie with Robbie. "Nothing," he said, then frowned. "I take it you like Monty Python?"

"Some dude I dated for a while introduced me to 'em. He's long gone, but we'll always have *The Life of Brian.*" She started softly singing the refrain from "Always Look on the Bright Side of Life," only to interrupt herself to say, "Hey—while you're up, how 'bout you make us some more popcorn? Since the dog ate most of the first batch."

Annabelle looked over, chewing and wagging her tail. On a sigh, Aidan went into the kitchen and did as he'd been told. But only because he wanted popcorn, too.

"The Python collection was June's," he said. "As were most of the DVDs."

"All those Britcoms?"

"Yes." He ripped the cellophane off the package, stuck it in the microwave and punched the timer. "I'm the one from the other side of the pond, but she couldn't get enough of British comedy." He crossed his arms, staring at the revolving turntable. "Especially when she was so sick. The more off-the-wall they were, the more she loved them." He turned to Winnie, who'd shuffled over, the quilt tightly wrapped around her shoulders, to climb up on a bar stool on the other side of the breakfast bar. "She used to say she was determined to die laughing."

Winnie smiled slightly, then sighed. "Unlike my grandmother, whose mission was clearly to make everyone as miserable as she was." She clutched at the quilt when it started to slip, the movement making him realize which one it was. Winnie caught his glance, guilt slashing across her face, even though she couldn't possibly have known what he was thinking. "I'm sorry…if you don't want me to use this—"

"No, it's fine. That's what she made it for."

Winnie's lips parted, as though she was about to say something, then changed her mind.

"What?"

"Forget it, you already think I'm crazy as it is."

"Then you've nothing to lose, I suppose."

"Good point," she said, smiling. "Okay, I swear I can feel June in the quilt. Like I'm being hugged by a person, not just a bunch of fabric and batting."

Aidan turned away. To take the popcorn out of the microwave. Find another bowl. Distract himself from remembering that the quilt had been on his and June's bed, that he'd hauled it to the loft after her death because sleeping under it alone—even looking at it—had hurt too damn much. That looking at it now, around Winnie's shoulders, wasn't bothering him nearly as much as he would have expected. "So who's minding the store while you're gone?"

"Wow. Talk about your non sequiturs."

"Sorry." The popcorn dumped into the bowl, he set it on the counter between them. "I'm not at my conversational best at two a.m."

"You have a conversational best?"

Winnie had no idea that her gentle teasing was more seductive than the sexiest negligee. A fantasy Aidan suddenly realized he was not above entertaining. Yes, about the static-haired woman currently wearing a quilt and, from what he could tell, a pair of sweats probably older than their owner.

"I can make conversation," he said, stuffing a fistful of popcorn into his mouth. "Intelligent conversation, even. When I have a mind to. And when it's not some ungodly hour. And I believe I asked you a question."

"And I believe that's called conversation." When he sighed, she grinned and said, "Elektra. I mentioned her before. E's been there since, gosh, long before I arrived on the scene. If you ask me, Ida wouldn't've had a shot in hell of keeping the place goin' if it hadn't've been for E. My grandmother wasn't exactly what you'd call a people person."

"So I gathered. How on earth did she end up with a restaurant?"

"Some relative or other apparently left it to her when he died," she said, cramming more popcorn into her mouth. "For reasons known only to Ida, she hung on to it."

Aidan pulled two cans of root beer out of the refrigerator and handed one to Winnie. "In some ways, your gran sounds like a woman after my own heart."

A handful of popcorn halfway to her mouth, Winnie frowned. "There you go again."

"There I go again, what?"

"Oh, please…you might fancy yourself a curmudgeon,

but you forget I saw you with Tess today. And Flo. And trust me, Ida would have never done what you did. Taking Tess and Miguel in, I mean. Down deep," she said, popping the tab on her soda, "*you're* a nice guy."

Aidan got the inference, was far too tired to refute it. "I take it you basically grew up in the diner?"

Smirking, Winnie caught a dribble of root beer with her thumb and licked it off. "Ida made it very clear I 'owed' her my services in return for a roof over my head. I did whatever needed doing—waiting tables, runnin' the register, cooking when I got old enough. Cleaning. When I wasn't in school, that is. I'll give the old girl one thing, she insisted I get my high school diploma." She took another sip of the soda, quietly burped. "Mainly because she couldn't stand the thought of her grand-daughter bein' some loser high school dropout. Of course, then I got pregnant, which shot her image all to hell, anyway. At least the graduation gown covered the baby bulge. Mostly."

"And…afterward?" Aidan ventured, knowing she'd understand.

Winnie tossed another popcorn kernel into her mouth. "She never let me forget my 'lapse.' Never."

"But she let you go to college."

That got a dry laugh. "Ida didn't *let* me do anything that didn't serve her own purposes. For my degree, I have to thank one of the old girl's many doctors, who was married to the daughter of the one of the town bigwigs, who in turn nagged the old woman something terrible about how I needed to continue my education. Wasn't until *Ida* decided, however, that my doing so would somehow 'cleanse' me of my past sins—and thus repair *her* image—that she conceded."

"Y'know, I'm seriously beginning to detest that woman," he said.

Winnie's lips curved, just slightly. "So much for being a woman after your own heart."

"I might have been wrong about that," Aidan said, then added over Winnie's soft chuckle, "So what're you going to do with the diner now that you own it?"

"I dunno. Haven't gotten that far in my thinking yet."

"Perhaps you could sell it."

"Right. Name me one person who'd want some run-down diner/gas station out in the middle of nowhere. And I can't just quit it, there's people there depending on their jobs." Then, frowning, she sharply shook her head. "But hey—this is my problem, not yours. So don't worry about it, okay?"

Aidan opened his mouth to say of course he wasn't worrying about it, only to realize just how close he'd edged to being, well, at least *concerned*. Then he shocked the hell out of himself by asking, "And were there boyfriends?"

Although Winnie nearly choked on her drink, there was laughter in her eyes when she lifted them to him. But the humor faded when she said quietly, "What there were, were unrealistic expectations. On both sides. More than once. And if you don't mind I'd like to leave it at that, okay?"

Unaccountably irritated, Aidan changed the subject. "So you've never used your degree?"

She shook her head. "Right about the time I graduated, all of Ida's threats to get really sick one day finally took hold. It started with her feeling less and less like coming into the diner, and she insisted I keep tabs on the business. Even after I was nursing her nearly full-time, except for when she'd let somebody come sit with her for a few hours so I could go into work."

"You were taking care of your grandmother *and* running a business?"

"It's amazing how much you can accomplish if you don't sleep." Her mouth flattened. "Guess that came out a little bitter, huh?"

"For God's sake, Winnie—why wouldn't it?" At the sudden sharpness to his tone, Winnie's eyes darted to his. "I'm torn between admiring you for your fortitude and wantin' to thrash you for not standing up for yourself more than you did. Or didn't Ida have the resources to pay for outside care?"

She almost smiled. "She could've had private nurses 'round the clock, if she'd wanted. And I could've forced the issue, if *I'd* wanted. I chose to take care of my grandmother, Aidan."

"*Why,* for the love of God?"

"Because…she didn't have anyone else, I suppose. Because she needed me. And nobody else on earth did."

Aidan realized he wasn't breathing properly, that not since the doctor'd told them that last round of chemo hadn't worked had he been this flat-out angry. "Your glass-half-full philosophy at work again, I suppose."

Her headed tilted. "Wow. Somebody sounds real ticked off."

"Dammit, Winnie—y'deserve better. You deserve… your own life. You deserve…" He paused, his heart hammering, knowing he was poised at the head of a path he'd thought to never go down again. "You deserve whatever makes *you* happy," he said, taking that first, frightening step. And then another. "And your gran should've been about helping you get there. At least before she got sick. I can't imagine…" He shook his head. "I can't imagine stifling Robbie, preventin' him from pursuing his own dreams. And I can't for the life of me figure out how you came out of that experience unscathed."

She barked out a soft, but brittle, laugh. "I'm hardly unscathed, Aidan! There were plenty of times I resented Ida with everything I had in me, times when I was so tired I was numb, when had to ask God's forgiveness when I'd be rearranging her pillows—again—and think how easy it would be to put both the old bat *and* me out of our miseries. But somewhere along the way, I decided that doing good, *being* good—" she yawned, covering her mouth with the back of her hand "—would in the long run make me feel better about myself."

"And did it?"

"Yeah. It did. Although—" she yawned again "—my motives weren't entirely noble, either. Because to be perfectly honest part of the reason I stuck by Ida was because I harbored some small hope of finally gaining her approval."

Aidan's heart cracked, along a fissure far less mended than he'd thought. "Did it work?"

"If you count her leaving me everything she had, I guess so. And I know we're supposed to do good for its own sake, not looking for anything in return, but…but just once it might've been nice to hear a 'thank you,' y'know? Oh, God…I must be more tired than I thought, I'm sounding like a real sad sack." She slid unsteadily off the bar stool. "You mind if I spend the rest of the night on the sofa? Because of that branch?"

"Not a'tall. Although why not sleep in the guest room? Tess won't be using it until tomorrow."

"Forget it, I already made the bed up for her, damned if I'm gonna change the sheets twice in twenty-four hours." After another enormous yawn, she turned, wobbling slightly on her way back to the sofa, where she curled up and instantly fell asleep under the quilt, the movie still paused on the TV. Annabelle jumped up to coil at her feet, her snout on her mistress's thigh, keeping watch.

For several moments, Aidan stood watching her, as well, frozen. Nonplussed. Terrified. She was just a woman, for God's sake. A mere human being of the female persuasion. And an aggravating one at that. Why, then, this insane compunction to reach back into her past and smooth it out? To somehow order her future so that all, or at least most, of her wishes came true?

Rattled far more than he wanted to admit, he walked over to turn off the TV, Annabelle's tail swishing when he shifted the quilt to cover Winnie's shoulders in the chilly room. Impulsively, he smoothed a stray hair off her cheek, anger surging up to flatten the wave of tenderness.

Because he was too damn close to letting her get to him.

To caring again.

And that, he thought as he shut the kitchen light and went back upstairs, would never do.

Chapter Nine

At least having a new baby around, Winnie groggily mused as she layered honey ham and hot pepper cheese atop whole wheat bread for lunch, didn't leave much time for thinking too hard about moody Irishmen with fiery eyes who'd get all outraged for your sake one day—or night, actually—only to then avoid you like Ebola for the next two. What really chapped her hide, though, was that he'd been the one to go poking around in her past, asking her all those questions about her grandmother and boyfriends and what all. So what the hell?

Add that to the fact that every minute longer she spent with Robbie was like pouring salt in a newly opened wound, and her good humor was being severely tested. Except then she'd remind herself that she'd never believed in a God who liked to toy with His creation, taunting His children with things they couldn't have—a view of life that had saved her sorry butt more often than not, otherwise she'd've probably tossed in the towel ages ago. Which meant if she'd been led here for a purpose, then she'd best be keeping her eyes and heart open for the good in it, hadn't she?

So, smartly steering her thoughts away from Mr. Grumpy, and even further away from the envious prickles brought on by watching Tess with her children, she asked the young mother—who was snuggled into a corner of the sofa with little Julia while Miguel played with Robbie's vast collection of Matchbox cars on the floor at her feet— how she was feeling.

"I can actually sit without wincing today," the brunette replied, dimples flashing when she smiled. "So that's progress, yes?" Then she laughed. "And God knows I'm doing better than Aunt Flo."

Lord, wasn't that the truth? Since Flo—who was thankfully napping in her room—refused to take her pain meds after the first day, she'd been cranky as all get-out and didn't care who knew it. Especially when she discovered she couldn't get her jeans zipped without assistance.

"I sure miss Rico, though," Tess said on a breath as she toyed with the sleeping baby's hand, reminding Winnie that nobody's life was perfect.

"When's he coming home?"

"Not until April. If they don't extend his tour again." She paused, staring fixedly at the baby, then said, "It's a bear, holding my breath all the time."

"I can imagine."

Another few seconds passed before, with another smile, Tess said, "I've got serious postpartum brain, so I don't know if I've told you how insanely grateful I am for all your help. You've really gone above and beyond." With a laugh, she added, "You fit right into the madness."

"I'll take that as a compliment," Winnie said, grinning, then she glanced up at the clock. When she'd asked Aidan

at breakfast what time he'd wanted lunch, he'd grumbled
something about not bothering herself on his account.
Which she'd translated as not bothering *him*.

Flo had already told her how he hated being bugged
when he was working, that he needed plenty of uninterrupted time to commune with his muse or whatever. And
it wasn't that Winnie didn't respect that, she thought as she
brazenly set off to flush the hermit out of his lair, but the
man still had to eat, for heaven's sake.

His studio was set off from the house proper by means
of a glassed-in breezeway, the forest on one side, spectacu-
lar views of the valley—through the milling egg factory—
on the other. The prone Annabelle, who'd discovered the
warm, terra-cotta floor their first day in residence, barely
acknowledged Winnie's presence as she passed.

The door to the studio was ajar, leaking cool light, some
sort of classical music and the tangy, rich smell of paint
and turpentine.

"Aidan?" she called, knocking.

No response. She cautiously pushed the door open,
steeling herself for growls and fang-baring, instead finding
herself alone in a large, light, very messy room, the dull
paint-splotched wooden floor stacked with canvases in no
particular order that she could tell. Over the swell of violins
and some caterwauling diva, a draft chilled her face, apparently from a half-open door across the room.

Acutely aware she was trespassing, Winnie scurried
across the floor, not even noticing the paintings. Not that
she much cared, since what she knew about art you could
write on a matchbook. The door opened onto a patio of sorts
halfheartedly covered in flagstone, on which sat a couple
of mismatched patio chairs and a small, rusty table. Aidan,
however, was nowhere in sight. Pulling her unzipped
hoodie closed over her cami, she called again. Nothing.
Fine, starve for all I care, she thought, returning inside.

Only to choke on her own spit.

The landscape was hair-raisingly massive, the jagged face of the mountains at sunset ablaze against the roiling gray-blue of the storm-soaked sky behind, the clashing colors colliding in enormous, crude swathes of thick paint.

Wow, Winnie thought. *So that's where all the testosterone went—*

"What are you doing here?"

Startled, Winnie spun around, her heart knocking at Aidan's livid green eyes, those of an animal whose territory has been invaded. He was wearing a ragged, no-color sweatshirt and jeans, both smeared with paint; he'd actually shaved two days ago, but the beard haze was back again. "I just came to tell you lunch was ready."

"And I told you not to bother."

Winnie ignored him. Instead, she twisted back to the canvas, perversely wanting to jolt him out of his bad mood. Even more perversely wanting another glimpse of the man who'd thrown mushrooms at her, who'd gone to bat for her at two in the morning. "Wow. What's it called?"

"Sunset over the Jemez."

"Oh. I was thinking something more along the lines of, I don't know…Angry Sex?"

"What?"

She turned, taking no small satisfaction in his startled expression. "Sorry. But that's the first thing that came to mind when I saw it."

It took a while, but at long last something like bemusement replaced the muddle of anger and annoyance and shock. A large, paint-smudged hand streaked through clean, soft, shaggy hair, and Winnie's own hand tingled in response.

"Y'really do just blurt out whatever's on your mind, don't you?"

"I find it saves people the trouble of guessing what I'm thinking."

Now he looked like he was trying so hard to keep a straight face it was all Winnie could do not to go right on over and tickle the daylights out of him. Somehow, though, she doubted Aidan would have taken the gesture in the spirit in which it was intended. Then, squinting at the painting, he sighed. "They all look like that these days."

"Like angry sex?"

"I hadn't actually articulated it to that degree, but yes." Then that brooding gaze slid to hers and she got goose bumps all the way down to Funland. Well, hell. "Thank God my clients aren't nearly as insightful as you are."

"Oh, I don't know," she said, thinking, *And you just had to go find him for lunch, didn't you?* "I can think of worse things than getting turned on by a painting. Puts a whole new spin to the concept of erotic art, though, doesn't it?"

But apparently the moment of quasi-levity had passed, the Soul Suckers having returned to drag Aidan back to Grumpville. She knew it was wrong to be aggravated with him, that a person can't help what he feels, but she was pissed all the same.

"Dammit, Aidan—you've gotta stop this."

He turned his frown on her. "Stop what?"

"Blowing hot and cold. Especially the cold part. Not only is it irritating as all hell, but it's totally unfair to Robbie. And don't you dare give me the I'm-an-artist-I'm-allowed-to-be-moody line, because I'm not buying it."

Aidan should have known better than to think that simply avoiding Winnie would end the torment of wanting what he knew he couldn't have. And not just the friction of two naked bodies warming each other—although the thought had disturbed his sleep more than once over the last two nights—but her indomitable spirit and strength and honesty, intent on warming his deadened soul. If not scorching it beyond recognition.

"And maybe some of us can't be Little Mary Sunshine all the time."

She crossed her arms, glowering, and he refused to react to how the pool of light from the skylight glanced off her shiny hair and caressed her shoulders and breasts and long legs and most of all made him all too aware of those ingenuous eyes, so much like Robbie's.

Made him all too aware how long he'd been since he'd touched a woman.

"And there's a difference between dealing with your pain and inviting it to move in indefinitely. I swear, Aidan, it's like you're afraid to allow yourself to be happy. Like you've decided what the hell, life sucks so you may as well give up."

Breathing hard, Aidan looked at the painting, at all that that frustrated, furious sexual energy pulsing on the canvas. Only June had known how much his work had always aroused him; only June had understood that—even though he'd found the process itself akin to foreplay, the completion of a project almost orgasmically satisfying—to describe it in physical terms alone didn't even begin to do it justice.

Only June had had the guts to call him on his mood swings, the patience to cajole him out of them. For another woman to have the same guts—

"You don't know me," he bit out. "You don't know me a'tall."

"You'd be surprised," Winnie said, and his gaze swung to hers, and loneliness and long-suppressed need slammed into him so hard his hands fisted at his sides. She couldn't possibly know why he'd sequestered himself in his studio so much these past two days, how that hearing her laughter, watching her with the baby and Miguel and Robbie had become nearly unbearable.

Oh, Aidan had placated his dying wife with lame reassurances that he'd at least be open to the idea of eventually finding someone else, even though he'd known even then how unlikely it would be to find a second person who'd "get" him the way June had. Winnie's relentless determination to see her cup as half full was bad enough; her even more relentless cheerfulness was about to drive him mad. But that she so immediately, and effortlessly, zeroed in on the one thing that most made Aidan who he was…

"I can't change who I am," he said, refusing to look at her, "just to please you."

"This has nothing to do with *me*," she said, sounding surprised. "I'm not even going to be around in a few days. But like I said, for Robbie's sake—"

His eyes snapped to hers. "And you're overstepping."

"Well, somebody sure as hell has to," she said, unperturbed, shoving her hands into her pockets. "Look, when you and June came to meet me before I had the baby, I'm sure I probably seemed pretty out of it. But just because I was angry and confused and scared, that didn't mean I wasn't paying real close attention to the two of you, trying to get a feel for what you were like deep down. The kind of parents you'd be—"

"I know that—"

"I'm not finished. What I'm sure you didn't know was that I had an actual list of qualities I was looking for—"

"Like being rich?"

"Nooo," she said with exaggerated patience. "And you're interrupting again. I'm talking about things like kindness. Integrity. A giving nature. But you know what was at the top of that list?" When he shook his head, she said, "A sense of humor. I wanted to know my baby would grow up in a house full of laughter. Like I had when my parents were alive. We might've been next door to dirt poor, but at least Mama and Daddy gave me that.

"What I remember most about that visit," she continued,

"aside from how kind the two of you were, is how easily both of you laughed. I know June's death knocked you flat on your butt," she said quietly, "but it's high time you get up and go find that person you used to be. Take your frustrations out on your paintings all you want, but not on Robbie. And not on yourself. Because I'm thinking it's a pretty safe bet he wants his old daddy back—"

"I *tried,* Winnie," Aidan shot back. "The night you made pizza, I tried to get him to open up to me, and he wouldn't. So what d'you suggest I do now?"

"Try harder," she said, then walked away, taking with her that generosity and good humor and straightforwardness that reminded him so acutely of what life had once been like, before a bunch of rampaging, mutant cells had made him all too aware of just how cruelly capricious that life could be.

All of which was putting Aidan into even more of a fouler than he'd been before she'd come.

In four days, Winnie Porter had managed to turn his world on its bloody head…just as June had done, all those years ago. But he was older now, far better able to control his impulses, and his hormones, than the painfully young man who'd fallen, almost instantly, for the woman with whom he'd spend the next fifteen years of his life.

But at twenty-three, he'd not only been powerless against the forces drawing him to June, he'd embraced the insanity with open arms. That it had worked out as well as it had certainly hadn't been due to any conscious, or conscientious, thought process on his part. Pure dumb luck, more like. But still, what the hell did he know then about risk? About loss?

About pain?

Aidan's stomach growled. Mutinously. He looked toward the door, practically hearing June's not-so-gentle chiding about his chronic stubbornness.

His boot heels slammed against the tiles so hard as he stormed through the breezeway, he half expected to leave a trail of sparks in his wake. When he came into the kitchen, Winnie looked up from behind the breakfast bar, her initial surprise yielding to a welcoming, guileless grin, reminding him of another smile he'd been unable to resist.

A smile he still missed every day of his life.

Then he blinked, and it was only Winnie's smile he saw. Only Winnie's smile that tempted, teased, taunted, and he wished with all his heart he could turn back the clock five days, before the blasted woman had entered the picture, with her blasted smile and her blasted good humor and her blasted refusal to see him for who he really was—the bitter bastard who, as his mother liked to say, regularly frequented the venerable establishment of Cross and Grump, Ltd.

He heard June's laughter so clearly she might've been right in the room with him.

By the time lunch was got through, however, Aidan realized he needed to get much farther away from the madness than his studio. As luck would have it, all three ladies started in on how they needed this, that and the next thing. Aidan jumped at the chance to go to the store for them.

A move that provoked near shock on the part of his housekeeper. "Since when did you overcome your allergy to shopping?"

"Since I have to pick up Robbie, anyway," he said, avoiding Winnie's gaze as he collected assorted lists, stuffing them into the pocket of his denim jacket. "I'll take Miguel, as well, shall I? Leave you women to it."

Unfortunately, he soon discovered, as the truck lurched and jolted down the hill, that he might have left the women, but two of the women—one dead, one very much alive— hadn't left him. In fact, they were going on at him in his head like a pair of magpies. So he did what any borderline insane man would do and turned on his radio to drown out the voices, singing lustily, and horrendously, along with Johnny Cash, making Miguel laugh and cover his ears. And Aidan got to thinking about laughter, about how it could lift a person up out of himself, like a balloon, floating over the rough spots of life. About how June would laugh until she cried, which only made her laugh all the harder. About Winnie's purposeful search for ways to bring it into her life.

But balloons would burst, wouldn't they? And then you crashed. So all in all, far safer for a person to stay down where they couldn't fall. Right?

Aidan could just imagine the look June would have given him. He felt a flicker of shame, that if his wife had refused to give in to the disease's constant efforts to destroy who she was, what the hell was he on about? *Give me a freaking break,* he could hear say…

And wouldn't Winnie join in with a *You said it, sister.*

Then *he* laughed, from the absurdity of it all, if nothing else. Not a big one, just a chuckle, but enough to make Miguel say, "What's so funny?"

Aidan smiled at the little boy. "Nothing," he said, reaching over to lightly cuff the lad on the back of his head.

They picked up Robbie, who, overcome with delight at the prospect of scoring more ice cream, immediately drew the younger boy into his nefarious plan. The two had become thick as thieves over the past couple of days, and not for the first time Aidan felt a slight pang of regret that he and June hadn't adopted more children.

The truck's tires crunched gravel as they pulled into Garcia's car park; before Aidan cut the engine, a bright red pickup even larger than his pulled up two spaces over. An instant later Rachel Griego climbed out in a flurry of long dark hair and teenage angst to stomp inside, her backpack slung on one shoulder. If the gods were kind, her father Johnny wouldn't notice Aidan, wouldn't wave, wouldn't push open his own door and climb down from his truck...wouldn't make a beeline for Aidan, who finally realized he was trapped.

"Hey, Johnny!" Robbie yelled, scrambling out of the truck and around the front to slap hands with the nearest approximation to a male friend Aidan had allowed himself to make since moving to Tierra Rosa. A friend he hadn't run into in months. Nor made any effort to run into.

But Johnny Griego was apparently not easily put off by grouchy Irishmen. As far as Aidan could tell, the horse breeder and trainer had always seemed content enough to take Aidan as he'd found him, even though Aidan had more than once found the other man's gregariousness irritating as all hell.

"Holy...smokes," Johnny now said, dark eyes alight over a broad grin. He thrust out his hand to give Aidan's a brief, hard shake, his barely average height belying a toughness honed from years of working horses. "I was beginning to think you'd dropped off the face of the earth, man, and here I see you in town twice in a week."

Aidan frowned. "You saw me?"

"Yeah, in Garcia's the other morning. You were with some blonde." He ruffled Robbie's hair. "So what earth-shattering event brings you down from your mountain to mingle amongst us mere mortals?"

"Females with lists," Aidan muttered, digging said lists out of his pocket.

"Fe*males?* Plural?"

Play nice, somebody said, Aidan wasn't sure who, as he said, "Flo sprained her wrist just as Tess went into labor." Standing on the seat behind the steering wheel, Miguel wrapped his arms around Aidan's shoulders from behind. With a grunt, he swung the little boy around to gently set him on the ground. "So I'm playing nursemaid for a week or so until one or both is back on her feet."

Johnny's grin turned devilish, reminding Aidan a lot

more of the handsome young cowboy he'd first met when they'd moved here than the fortyish—although still handsome, Aidan supposed—man in front of him. "Oh?"

"I've got help," Aidan put in, only to immediately think, *And how do you intend to explain this one?*

"The blonde?"

Aidan flinched. "How'd you—?"

"It's a small town," Johnny said with a shrug. "Word gets around. As does your guest. Nice gal, from everything I hear. What's her name again?"

"Her name's Winnie!" Robbie put in, face aglow. "She knows how to make pizza! And fudge!"

"A woman worth her weight in gold," Johnny said, chuckling. Then he looked back at Aidan. "What everyone's wondering, though, is why on earth anybody'd *choose* to visit Tierra Rosa. I mean—" he removed his cowboy hat to run a hand through his thick, dark hair, just beginning to gray at the temples "—we're not exactly the most popular tourist destination on the map, are we?"

"Something about an article in a magazine," Aidan said with a shrug of his own, then angled himself toward the porch. "You going in?"

"Me? Nah, just dropping Rach off from school." Aidan noticed the cloud that darkened the other man's normally sunny features, but since he wasn't one for prying, he left it be. He knew Johnny and his wife—a journalist or some such—had been divorced since their daughter was a toddler, vaguely remembered overhearing something about the girl's going back and forth between the two, whenever her mother's schedule permitted. More than that, however, he didn't know. And had no interest in asking. It was exhausting, caring about people.

"Dad?" Robbie asked, tugging at his sleeve. Aidan lowered his gaze. "Are we *ever* gonna go riding again?"

"Sure," Aidan said, his smile tight. "Some day." But

when he tried to make his escape with a "Great running into you, Johnny," the other man said, "Actually, I need to talk to you. About the horses. You got a minute?"

He could put the man off, he supposed. Just as he'd put off almost everything else that hadn't been absolutely essential to the settling of June's affairs, or his son's well-being, for the past year. But what would be the point, since the subject would only come up again later?

With a faint smile, Aidan turned to Robbie. "Why don't you take Miguel inside and see about that ice cream?" After the boys rushed inside—in direct violation of the warning sign in the window—Aidan faced Johnny again. Saw the combination of sympathy and concern in his deep brown eyes.

"The horses are okay, aren't they?"

"Yeah, yeah, they're fine," Johnny said, bracing the sole of one cowboy boot on the porch lip. "Physically, anyway. Any animal I board's gonna be treated as well as my own."

"Then what's the problem?"

"You know damn well what the problem is. We try to ride 'em now and again, but it's not the same as you or the boy coming out like you used to. The horses miss you."

Having spent his entire childhood around horses, Aidan knew better than to argue. Still… "I've lost my taste for riding, that's all."

"And it's not like I don't understand. But Robbie…he's a natural. More than my own kid ever was, that's for sure. Seems a shame to nip a talent like that in the bud."

Aidan scrubbed a hand over his mouth, his beard stubble scraping his palm. "I'll bring him out soon, then. I promise."

"And what about you?" When Aidan didn't reply, Johnny said, "Look, I got this customer asking about Maggie. He's looking for a big, well-broke horse for his daughter who's fourteen and already five-eleven—"

"Maggie's not for sale," Aidan snapped. "And neither is Strike, before you ask. Or the pony."

"Aw, hell, Aidan—you haven't even been out to see them since…for more than a year. Don't get me wrong, you're free to board 'em with me as long as you like, but it kills me to see 'em neglected. If you ask me, far better to sell 'em to somebody who'll appreciate them. And you know I'd only recommend a buyer I was a hundred percent sure would do right by 'em—"

"They're not for sale," Aidan snapped. "And I'll hear no more talk about it. Is that clear?"

Johnny calmly folded his arms across his denim jacket and looked Aidan straight in the eye. "Perfectly. And like I said, you know I'll take as good care of them as I know how. But if you don't mind my saying…" He took a deep breath. "Hell, nobody knows more'n me how hard it is to get back into the swing of things after something like this happens. But life does go on, buddy—"

"My wife *died,* Johnny! Long before I was ready for her to go."

The other man's face darkened. "And when your heart's ripped out, it don't much matter how it happens—the pain's the same. So don't go thinking you've got the market cornered on grief, okay? And for damn sure you don't want to let that grief mess up your kid. He loved to ride, Aidan. *You* loved to ride. And so did June. So damn it— what good's it doing anybody to deny you or your kid something that made you *happy?*"

"*Made* me happy, Johnny. Past tense."

Johnny's gaze warred with his for a moment before he shook his head, then walked back to his truck, climbed in and drove off.

"Dad?" Robbie said, poking his head out the door. "Miguel wants to get some ice cream for his mom, too. Is that okay?"

"Sure," Aidan said, trying to shake off the conversation as he went inside, grabbed a basket and started tossing items into it.

Except, like a stubborn burr, the conversation wouldn't shake.

"Wonder what bug's up his butt?" Flo muttered to Winnie when Aidan finally returned, nearly two hours later. Standing on the other side of the breakfast bar chopping onions for spaghetti sauce, she glanced at Aidan striding across the room toward them, then back at Flo.

"Why do you think there's a bug up his butt?" she whispered.

"Jus' look at his face."

"Am I supposed to be seeing a difference?"

"Okay, so it's subtle. But trus' me. He's pissed."

Sure enough, when Aidan reached the kitchen and started unloading plastic bags, he did seem more animated than usual. Then he suddenly turned to Winnie and said, "D'you ride?"

"What?"

"Do you ride? Horses," he added irritably, like she was hopelessly slow. And if he hadn't looked so impossibly frustrated—although about what, she couldn't begin to imagine—and if she hadn't become used to his brusqueness, she might have taken offence. But it would've been like taking offense at a frightened dog's growl.

"It's been a while, but yeah—"

"Western?"

"What else?"

"Good. I've got horses boarding at a ranch near here, they need to be ridden. We'll take the boys with us so Flo and Tess won't have to worry about them. Day after tomorrow," he added as an afterthought, then stomped out of the kitchen through a sea of discarded plastic bags.

Winnie turned to Flo. "He's got horses?"

When Flo turned, she had tears in her eyes. "Him and Miss June, they used to go riding nearly every weekend. There's a pony for Robbie, too. But since Miss June got too sick to ride, the boss hasn't rode, neither. Not even once. Hasn't even gone out to see the horses, far as I know."

"Oh," Winnie said, followed by a second, more meaningful "Oh!" when she realized just how monumental this was. Except…

"I'll be right back."

She found him on the back deck, glowering at the beginnings of the sunset.

"Back where I come from," she said, making him turn around, "it's the custom to *ask* a woman if she'd like to do something. Like go riding, for instance. So." She crossed her arms. "Care to try this again?"

Aidan looked back out toward the setting sun. "I'm thinking of going horseback riding on Saturday. Wouldya be interested in goin' along?"

"I'd love to," she said, then turned smartly on her heel and walked away.

Chapter Ten

"You know," Winnie said pleasantly a few feet away, rocking back and forth on June's massive mare as the horses plodded laconically along the sun-dappled forest path, "you could at least *look* like you're havin' fun."

From atop Strike, one arm holding Miguel securely in front of him, Aidan glanced over, catching the wicked humor flashing in her eyes from underneath a broad-brimmed hat. He looked front again. "I'm having a fine time. Can't you tell?"

"Could've fooled me," she said, then winced slightly when the horse navigated a slight incline on the trail. "Oh, Lord...I am gonna regret this tomorrow. I'm feeling things stretch I'd forgotten even existed."

"We'll take it easy, then," Aidan said, annoyed to feel the ping of awareness at the unintentional double meaning. He shifted slightly to tuck a softly singing Miguel more firmly against his stomach. Annabelle darted out of the

KAREN TEMPLETON   143

undergrowth, covered in weed fluff and twigs, woofed joyously and darted back in. "Wasn't planning on doing anything too strenuous with the kids along, anyway."

And indeed, the path was beyond tame, gently zigzagging up the mountainside to a clearing with a grand view where they'd have lunch before heading back. He could tell the poor horses were bored beyond belief, but for now it was more than enough for them. For him.

Fine, so he'd followed everyone's advice, forced himself out of himself for his child's sake, for the horses', having no idea how bloody hard it would be to watch another woman sit Maggie, how torn he'd feel when the mare immediately accepted Winnie, eagerly nibbling at the strands of gold that had escaped Winnie's lame attempt at putting up her hair…just as the horse had once done to a black-haired head, provoking the same delighted laughter.

Stirring in Aidan reactions so similar as to scare him to death.

In a hat and boots Aidan had been stunned to discover were nearly outgrown, Robbie rode slightly ahead of them on his dappled gray pony, Patches, also nearly outgrown. "Miguel! Rabbits!" Robbie called back, which of course scared the things off into the brush and provoked a gasp of wonder in the four-year-old…and a flurry of bittersweet warmth deep inside Aidan, as he remembered riding with Robbie when he was small and everything that memory evoked. Then he sighed, realizing that time passed, children grew, life continued, whether he was interested in playing along or not.

You got it, babe, he heard in his head. *Now what're you gonna do about it?*

Frowning, he swiveled his head, remembering he was supposed to be keeping an eye on Winnie, who hadn't ridden since her early teens when a long-since dead great uncle had bullied Winnie's grandmother into letting Winnie spend a month on his small ranch. The sun was warm, even up this high, warm enough that she'd shucked her overshirt, now tied around her waist, unbuttoned an extra button on her long-sleeved knit shirt. With her hair tucked up underneath her hat…

Funny, how he'd never noticed her long neck before this.

"You've a good seat," he said, looking away.

"I *beg* your pardon?"

"How you sit in the saddle. Your posture." His glaze flicked to hers again, then away. "You don't look like someone who's not sat a horse in fifteen years."

"Looks can be deceiving," she said, obviously mimicking him, then said, "How'd you come to ride?"

"My parents raise thoroughbreds. I was ridin' before I was walking."

He sensed her gaze settle on Robbie. "Robbie said he's only met them a few times."

The comment's off-handedness only seemed to emphasize the awkwardness of the situation, the enormously heavy secret hanging between them. "It's a long trip," he said. "And they're not much for traveling."

"You, either, I don't imagine."

"I did a lot, when I was younger, gettin' my career off the ground. But since Robbie came, not so much." Feeling her eyes on him, he smirked. "And you're thinking your 'why is he such a hermit?' thoughts again, I can tell."

"I thinking if I had the resources you do, I'd be on the nearest plane to anywhere."

"And where would you like to go, Winnie Porter?"

"Oh, wow…where do I start? Italy? Brazil? China…I'd *love* to see China someday. And go on a photo safari in Africa. And Ireland," she said, tossing him a grin that made him almost…something he couldn't imagine being again. "All that green must be *amazing*. But you know—" she inhaled deeply "—it's sure beautiful up here, too. Peaceful."

"I suppose."

"Aidan. For heaven's sake."

He frowned over at her. "What?"

But she only shook her head. Then she said, "It's been a long time since I've felt like this."

"Since when? This morning?"

For a moment or two, there was no sound save the plodding of the horses' hooves, Miguel's breathing, the buzz of a single engine plane overhead. Then Winnie said quietly, "I know my determination to stay positive irritates the life out of you, but I'd rather annoy people with my cheerfulness than join them down in the dumps."

"Your cheerfulness doesn't irritate me, Winnie," he said, irritably.

"You are too much," she said, that damn laughter sparkling in her voice as she adjusted her hat to better shield her eyes from the sun. "And anyway, there's a difference between being cheerful and feeling at peace."

"Which is?"

"Well, I suppose cheerfulness is something you can put on, like a bright piece of clothing, to make yourself and people around you feel better. I'm good at that," she said, shrugging at her own candor. "Peacefulness, however, is more a feeling that just sorta comes over you when you savor the moment. You can't make it happen. Although I suppose you can *let* it happen."

"I see," he said, although he really didn't. "And when was the last time you felt peaceful?"

"For longer than a couple of minutes?" She thought, then said, "When my parents were still alive, I guess. Not all the time, I don't mean that. I remember a lot of tension, too—I'm sure there were serious money problems, although they never came right out and said anything to me—but Mama and Daddy were real good at cherishing the good times. Mama, especially. Lord, that woman could milk more fun out of runnin' through the sprinklers on a god-awful hot summer day, or just sittin' outside on the porch and watching the stars, than anybody I've ever known." She shifted in her saddle. "And she loved like it was as easy and natural as breathin', too. Far as I was concerned there was no better role model in the world."

"Then you really are very like her."

Her gaze briefly swung to his, then back front, but it was some time before she said, "I think a lot of the time people are hard and mean because they don't know how to be anything else. Or they've forgotten."

"You're very generous," Aidan said quietly, hugging Miguel.

"Not really. I think it's more that I don't ever want bitterness to eat away at me like that—"

"Dad?" Robbie called over his shoulder. "C'n we stop soon? My legs're gettin' sore."

Aidan heard Winnie say "Bless you," under her breath as he shouted back, "We're just there, anyway. See that clearing up ahead?"

Once stopped, Aidan dismounted, then helped a giggling Miguel down to immediately run off with Robbie into the sparse woods beside the path.

"Watch out for snakes!" Aidan yelled after them, and Robbie yelled back, "I know, I know!" Then Aidan turned to Winnie, still astride the mare.

"Plannin' on staying up there through lunch?" Aidan said, loosely tethering Strike to a nearby live oak.

"Snakes?" she said, brows pulled down.

"Well, probably not so much this time of year. It's a bit cold for most of them. But it never hurts to remind the lads to keep an eye out."

"Fine. I'll keep an eye out from up here, thank you, you can just pass me a sandwich."

"You're afraid of snakes?"

"Yeah, it's this weird phobia I have about slithery,

sneaky creatures whose bites can cause excruciating death. But I'm not afraid of spiders, so do I get extra points for that?"

"Spiders are sometimes poisonous, too."

"They don't slither," she said, as though that explained everything. But he could see, behind the joking facade, that she was deadly serious.

"Shall I do a sweep, then? Make sure we're in a snake-free zone?"

"I'd appreciate it."

When he returned after said sweep, however, Winnie hadn't budged.

"You can come down now. It's safe. I promise."

"I'm not sure I can," she said, her mouth a flat line. "I think my legs are welded to the horse."

By rights, Aidan should have been beyond exasperated. Except between her initial genuine terror and her current chagrin at her predicament, all he could feel was…well, not exasperation, that was certain.

"Come on, then," he said, reaching for her waist. "Unhook your feet from the stirrups—"

"Yeah, I think I remember that part," she said dryly, even as she braced her palms on his shoulders so he could lift her down. Only her knees buckled the moment her feet touched the ground, so naturally Aidan grabbed her to keep her from falling, and he thought, *I will not be a party to a cheesy chick-flick setup,* about the same time Winnie apparently thought much the same thing because she tried to push away. Only Maggie—who normally never, ever moved once she'd been dismounted—shifted slightly to her left, nudging Winnie right back into his arms.

And, oddly, he wasn't nearly as ready to let go as he would have thought.

Even more oddly, neither apparently was Winnie. Although truth be told, she was a bit wedged between him and the horse, her arms tucked in so that her hands had no place to go but on his chest. And over the scent of horse, he inhaled hers, strong enough to taste, shampoo and soap and wood smoke...felt her stiffen, wary, her eyes questioning...and he smiled.

"Damn horse," he said softly.

She smiled back then, and he saw in her eyes—because she was too honest by half—that if he were to kiss her, she wouldn't resist.

Alarm streaking through him, he backed up, setting her free, and she lifted one eyebrow as if to say, *Got it.* Except she'd barely got ten feet away when her legs gave out on her and down she went, flat on her bum.

"Winnie!" Aidan yelled, rushing over at her howl. "Are you all right?"

Only by the time he—and the kids, and the dog— reached her, he realized she was howling, all right.

With laughter.

Just keep 'em laughin', Winnie thought, a half hour after her pratfall as she wended her way back from the small, glittering stream behind the clearing, wishing she could shake off the memory of that almost-kiss as easily as she shook water off her hands. While she *could* blame her wobbly knees on not being on a horse in a while, truth be told the horse hadn't had a whole lot to do with it.

And Lord knows the horse didn't have a blamed thing to do with her fluttery stomach and itchy lips and let's not even *think* about Funland, which was *this close* to offering Unlimited Rides passes.

Brother.

Behind her, the boys, with Annabelle's enthusiastic encouragement, continued to whoop and holler as they skipped stones across the water, routed out snoozing creatures—of the nonslithering variety—from under rocks.

Even though her legs were nearly back to normal, she gratefully collapsed onto the ground to prop her back against the trunk of a gnarled tree. Five or so feet away, Aidan leaned against his own tree, legs outstretched, feet crossed at the ankles, hands linked over his stomach, his face to the sun.

Thinking about the last time he'd been up here with June, she imagined, a thought that left her feeling far sadder than she had any right to feel. Because no matter how she looked at it, she was intruding. Doing exactly what she'd sworn not to do—

"I take it you've recovered, then?"

"Mostly." She glanced over at him. His eyes were still closed. "I didn't think you'd heard me."

"Are you kidding?" he said, almost smiling. "All that ruckus you made tramping t'rough the dry grass, they could probably hear you in Albuquerque."

She looked back toward the creek, Aidan's good-natured ribbing burning her ears. *Now* there's *the man I met all those years ago,* she thought, swatting away the testiness as she reached out to swipe a glob of mud off her knee. Then she glanced again at him and smiled herself.

"Don't look now, but you seem almost…peaceful."

"Trick of the light," he said, reaching up to scratch his bristly jaw, then folding his hands again. "It'll pass. By the way, I've been meanin' to ask you…what happened to all the earrings and nose rings and…things?"

"I grew out of my human pincushion phase."

He grinned. Dimples and all. "Any tattoos?"

"Are you kidding? I nearly fainted just getting a couple lousy holes in my nose and eyebrow. I may talk the talk, but inside I'm a huge wuss. When it comes to needles." She paused. "And snakes." Another pause. "Speaking of *by the way*… I'm really proud of you."

His brow puckered. "Proud?"

"This can't be easy for you. Coming up here. Me ridin' June's horse."

"It's something I needed to do," he said after a long moment, opening his eyes at last. "Whether I'd admit it or not. Funny, though," he said, rubbing his back against the tree trunk, "runnin' into Johnny Griego like that when I haven't seen him a'tall since June died. It's almost as if…" He shook his head, clearly determined to let the thought fall to the ground. Then he said, "But this can't be easy for you, either. Watching Robbie—"

"Sittin' where there be snakes."

"And you accuse *me* of blowin' hot and cold."

Her brow knotted, Winnie met his gaze. "What are you talkin' about?"

"One minute you're honest to a fault about your feelings, the next…" He shrugged, looking forward again. "Why is it so hard to simply admit our fears, for the love of Mike? The real ones, I mean."

Whoa.

"Maybe…we just have to find the right person to admit them to," she said. "Somebody we know we can trust. Like the snake thing. Somehow, I knew you wouldn't make fun of me about it."

She could feel his frown. "Why would I do that?"

"That's just it—*you* wouldn't. But most men…" Sighing, she leaned forward to wrap her arms around her knees. "I've been scared to death of snakes ever since I can remember. But I had to learn the hard way to keep it a secret from any of my so-called boyfriends, 'cause to a person they'd rag me about it something terrible. One jerk went so far as to leave this big old sucker in the front seat of my truck. It took Elektra two hours to calm me down afterward. From then on I swore I'd never tell another living soul about it."

"But you told me."

"Yeah. I told you." Her mouth pulled tight. "I know it's irrational to be so scared, but—"

"Phobias aren't irrational to the people sufferin' from them, Winnie," he said with no small amount of anger. "They can be overcome, but anybody who'd take advantage of your fears like that, especially someone purportin' to be a *man…*" Out of the corner of her eye, she saw his mouth pull into a grim line. "And anyway, where's it written we have to be brave about everything?" He paused. "Don't let this go to your head, but you're one of the bravest women I've ever met, Winnie Porter. A wuss, you are definitely not."

And if you keep talking like that, she thought, *I'm gonna fall in love with you, and then where would I be?*

She'd been with plenty of men who were wrong for her. Most, if she was being honest, had felt wrong right from the start. And the one or two who hadn't…well, she supposed she hadn't been all that surprised when they'd quickly turned out to be cheap imitations of the real thing, too.

But this man was the genuine article. Yeah, he had a couple screws loose, but who didn't? And anyway, loose screws just needed tightening, was all. The rest of him was solid as a rock. Exactly what she'd been wishing for, she realized with a sharp, achy jolt, even if she hadn't exactly had a list made out or anything. So here she was, sitting next to somebody who felt more right than any man she'd ever known…and who, without a doubt, couldn't have been more wrong. Then he said, "I've been considering how to go about tellin' Robbie the truth," and she nearly fell over.

"The truth? You mean about—?"

"Yes."

"When did you change your mind?"

"I don't suppose I ever really t'ought we could get away with keeping it a secret for long," he said, toying with a blade of long, dry grass. "Especially now that you've been around the lad so much." He looked over at her, the sun making him squint. "So it's down to a matter of the hows and whens. Which is the part I haven't figured out yet."

Feeling warmth flood through her, Winnie looked toward the stream. "I'll leave that part up to you. Although you do know I'm leaving day after tomorrow, right?"

"Day after tomorrow?"

"Flo's healing up pretty fast, and Tess said she's ready to go home. No reason for me to stick around."

She could feel his eyes on the side of her face, sensed when he turned and looked front, as well. "I'll let you know, then. What I decide."

"Good." Then she asked, "How did you and June meet?"

When several beats passed without his answering, she turned to see him looking at her like she'd clearly lost her marbles. "I t'ought this was supposed to be about moving on?"

"And when are you going to get it through your head that talkin' about somebody *is* moving on? Look, I'm…glad I've gotten to know you a little better. For Robbie's sake, y'know? So if June were here…"

I sure as hell wouldn't be falling in love with you.

"If June were still here, I'd like to get to know her better, too. That's all I'm saying. So." She picked up an abandoned apple from lunch and bit into it. "Ball's in your court, buddy."

This wasn't supposed to be happening, he wasn't supposed to feel this damn comfortable with her, wasn't supposed to feel…

Like this.

So do what she's asking, talk about June, let the memories wipe Winnie right out of your head.

"It was fifteen years ago," he started. "I was in Dublin, doin' the whole starving-artist routine." He reached up to rub the back of his neck. "My parents had basically disowned me because I'd chosen art over goin' into the horse-breeding business with my father."

"Oh, no…"

"We're reconciled now—Robbie did that—but it was definitely touch-and-go for some time. And why I said what I said t'other day about never suffocating the lad. Because I'd never do to a child of mine what my parents did in the name of 'wanting only the best' for me. Anyway…June and a girlfriend of hers were doing the grand tour of the British Isles, and I ran into her in a pub, believe it or not. To be honest, I didn't have much love for the Americans I'd met up to that point, but she was different. She was real, in a way I'd never known a woman to be real before. I felt a right fool, of course, when I realized the difference in our ages, but…"

He laughed softly. "For whatever reason, she never saw me as a boy. And I never really saw her as being any age a'tall." He looked at her. "Her friend continued on the tour. June didn't. We got married two weeks after we met."

"You're kidding?"

"Not a bit of it. Needless to say, my parents were right put out with me, even more than before. So you see, you've got nothin' on me, when it comes to bein' a rebel."

"No, I guess not." She crunched into her apple again and said around the bite, "So did you come back to the States right after?"

"We did. I'd been to New York and Boston a few times, but never to the west. I only knew what it was like from pictures. I'd never imagined the landscape could take a person's breath away like this, make you feel honored and insignificant at the same time. In an odd sort of way it reminds me of the Irish seacoast, where I grew up. The grandness of it, I suppose. The vastness."

"I know what you mean," Winnie said beside him, sighing. "You ever been to Texas?" When he shook his head, she laughed. "Now *that's* vast. Some people see it as a whole lotta nothin'. I see it as…uninterrupted." When Aidan sniggered, she looked at him. "I can't help seein' the upside of things, Aidan—"

"It's okay, I'm getting used to it." Against his better judgment, he let his eyes touch hers, let the scraps of who he used to be commune—for just a moment—with the vast, unfathomable goodness and honesty that was Winnie Porter, and he felt honored and insignificant and more tortured than he could ever remember feeling in his life. Her head tilted, ever so slightly, questions blooming in her eyes, and her lips parted—

Shrieks of laughter from down by the stream sent Aidan's thoughts tumbling and his head around as, moments later, boys and dog clambered up the rise, all parties wet and muddy and shivering and grinning.

"Annabelle shook water all *over* us!" Robbie said, barely able to stand for the giggling, and Aidan sucked in a breath, that a few minutes ago he'd made a promise that would in all likelihood rock his son's world, long before either Robbie or Aidan were ready to be rocked again. Then the thought came—*This is right*—and he relaxed, at least enough to let the breath out again.

"Yeah," Miguel put in, his head bobbing, smiling even more broadly than his new best friend. "We're *soaked*, man!"

Annabelle barked, clueless. And shook again, flinging mud *everywhere.*

Laughing, Winnie got up to dig dry clothes for both boys out of her saddle bag. "Something told me to bring extra clothes for you two," she said, the sun glinting off her hair as she tossed Robbie his clean duds, then got on her knees to quickly change Miguel out of his soggy shirt and jeans.

"Help!" came a muffled cry from a few feet away. "Somebody, *any*body! I'm *stuuuuck!*"

Aidan turned to Robbie, who was stumbling in circles,

headless, as he struggled out of his clammy hoodie. Laughter surging up from the dark pit that had been his soul for far too long, Aidan grabbed the drunken whirling dervish, yanking the hoodie off with one pull. Flushed, *happy,* Robbie grinned up at him.

"This has been the best day of my *life!*" he said, with the unthinking candor of the young, then—redressed— rushed off with Annabelle and Miguel on his next adventure. Aidan turned, watching Winnie watch the boys as they vanished, and he saw on her face a softened version of the expression he'd just seen on his son's.

"It's time we got back," he said, and her head whipped around.

Still smiling, she walked over to him, laid one hand on his arm to steady herself and stood on tiptoe to kiss him on his cheek. Then she turned, calling the boys and dog loud enough to startle birds from the trees.

Chapter Eleven

"Ohmigod, E…you *didn't?*"

"I sure as hell did, baby! I just made Andy check, to make sure my eyes weren't playin' tricks on me! Can you believe it—I won me *sixty thousand dollars!*"

Grinning for her friend, Winnie rolled over on the loft's futon—Aidan had whacked off the obnoxious limb the first day—letting E's good news wash over her in the near silence. The boys, worn out from their horseback adventures, had been dead to the world by nine; everybody else, including Aidan, had retired soon after, although she suspected Aidan wasn't asleep, either.

This had been *some* day.

"After all these years, Elektra," Winnie said, focusing on the angled beams overhead, barely visible in the ghostly glow from the single over-the-counter light from the kitchen. "Your mama's birthday finally paid off."

"But that's the weird thing," E said. "I didn't play

Mama's birthday. I was about to write the numbers in, like always, when suddenly a whole new set came to me outta nowhere. Real strong, like somebody was sayin' 'em right in my ear. Eleven, sixteen, nineteen, thirty, four."

Winnie's hand tightened around her phone. "What did you say?"

"Eleven, sixteen, nineteen, thirty, four. Why?"

"Ohmigod, E…. That's Miss Ida's birthday."

"*What?* Holy you-know-what…I think I just turned three shades lighter."

Nobody said anything for a good ten seconds, until E broke the silence with, "You think this is like, you know, some kind of message from the grave?"

"I'm thinking it's a really creepy coincidence, is what I'm thinking."

"You don't sound so sure. About it being a coincidence, I mean, I think we're in agreement on the creepiness thing."

Winnie sighed. "Honey, these days I'm not sure of anything. So what're you gonna do with all that cash?"

"I have no idea. I mean, it sounds like a lot of money—hell, it *is* a lot of money—but it's not like I can retire on it or anything. Invest it, I suppose…oh, hell, I don't know. Maybe you can help me figure it out when you get back?"

"Sure thing," Winnie said, smiling, stroking Annabelle's ruff. "Only a couple more days, I promise…"

She clapped shut her phone, tapping it to her lips for a moment before tossing it next to Annabelle, who was curled up in Winnie's shucked-off clothes on the floor beside the bed. For Aidan's and Robbie's sakes, she was pleased as punch that the day had wrought such miracles for them both, hauling the pair of them out of the depths of their grief. At least enough, she thought, that they'd be able to get on firm footing again. What the day had done for her, however…

Best not to think about that.

On the drive back from the horse farm—over the snores of Miguel, who'd passed out in his booster seat behind them—a very bubbly Robbie had asked her if maybe they could carve pumpkins the next day, with such earnestness she couldn't bear to say no. But the truth of the matter was all she wanted to do was get the hell out of there, before her heart disintegrated completely.

And if she'd had her druthers, if Flo and Tess had been just a *little* more on top of things, she and Annabelle would be history by now, their presence already fading into memories. Just like Robbie and Aidan would eventually fade for her.

Or so she told herself.

One more day, she thought, the back of her throat thick as she stared out the small window over the futon into the black, starry night. *One…more…day….*

"How's this look, Winnie?"

Robbie turned his half-carved pumpkin around so Winnie could see it, feeling a lot better when she smiled. Because ever since they'd gone riding, she hadn't been the same. She still laughed and stuff, and told funny stories, but now it seemed like she was *trying* to be funny, instead of just *being* funny.

"Oooh, spooky," she now said, smiling, dumping out another scoop of pumpkin guts into a big plastic bowl on the table. She had strings of gooey stuff and seeds all over her, but she didn't care. It was more'n a week before Halloween, and he knew the cut pumpkins would get all smushed in and yucky by then, but at least this way he got to carve them with Winnie.

He didn't like thinking about her leaving, but she'd already said there really wasn't any reason for her to stay longer. In fact, Dad and Flo, who was feeling much better, had just taken Tess and the baby and Miguel back to Tess's house. The house already felt empty; it was only gonna feel emptier once Winnie left.

And that kinda confused him. That he liked her so much. Maybe too much. From the way Dad kept looking at her, Robbie thought maybe he was feeling the same way. Like he liked having Winnie around, too, but he didn't like how much he liked it—

"Hey." Winnie touched his hand. "You okay?"

"Do you *hafta* go?" When she didn't say anything, Robbie looked over to see her staring real hard at her pumpkin, biting her lip.

"Yeah, honey," she finally said. "I do. I've got a business to run back in Texas, and I don't have a job here. I'm just here on vacation, remember?" Then she smiled. "But I'm tickled to death you want me to stay."

He felt his face get warm. "It's just been...funner since you've been here. And when we had everybody else around...it was like Christmas, sorta. But without the presents."

Winnie sat down, frowning at her blank pumpkin. She'd been so busy cleaning 'em out for Robbie she hadn't carved one of her own yet. "You know," she said as she picked up a black crayon and started drawing a face, "maybe that's it, maybe you should think of us being here like a holiday. Like a special time you know won't last forever, so you just enjoy it as much as you can."

"Yeah, well, I hate when it's not Christmas anymore, either."

"Okay, so maybe that's not the best way to look at it. Because you're right, January totally sucks. But then there's Valentine's Day—candy, *yaaaay!*" she said, waggling her hands up by her head. "And then Easter—more candy, *yaaaay!*—and then it's summer with the Fourth of July and fireworks, and suddenly it's Halloween, and Thanksgiving, and before you know it...it's Christmas again."

"I'm just a little kid," Robbie said. "Time moves like a snail for me."

Winnie burst out laughing. "You're one *amazing* little kid, is what you are. Where do you come up with this stuff?"

Robbie shrugged, pleased, as he sawed around a tooth in his pumpkin with a little tool he couldn't cut himself with. "Dunno. It's just the way my brain works, I guess. The baby was really cute, huh? At least when she wasn't screaming her head off. Miguel, too."

"And you were *so* good with him when he was here. A lot of big kids don't like it when littler kids hang around them, but you were great."

"I liked showing Miguel how to do stuff. It was like he was my little brother or something."

After a minute, Winnie said, "You'd be a good big brother, that's for sure."

"Yeah, maybe. Mom and Dad didn't want any more kids, though. They said they were happy with just me."

She gave him a funny little smile. "I'm sure they were."

"So when are you going again?"

"Tomorrow, sugar," she said softly.

"Bet you got a boyfriend back home, huh?"

She sputtered another laugh. "Nope, no boyfriend. Why do you ask?"

He shrugged. "Dunno. D'you like the Three Stooges?"

Now she grinned. "The Three Stooges are the *bomb*. I noticed you guys had a bunch of their movies."

"Yeah, they're Mom's. We usedta watch them together."

"Did your Dad watch them, too?"

"Sometimes. But I don't think they were his thing."

Winnie made this kinda choking sound in her throat. "No, I don't imagine so."

Robbie poked out a chunk of loose pumpkin from around the carved tooth. "Mom told me once, a long time ago, about how they picked me," he said, wondering why it took Winnie such a long time before she said, "Oh?"

* * *

Winnie had read somewhere that the average person has something like fifty thousand thoughts a day. Most kids, she'd long since decided, seemed determined to verbalize most of those thoughts, in purely random order—as evidenced by the number of parents traveling with young children who'd come into the diner with what Winnie called the Road Trip Zombie look. A condition she had no doubt Robbie could inflict in twenty seconds flat.

Except she had the definite feeling his subject switches weren't random at all. That, in fact, he'd been giving very careful consideration about not only what to bring up, but when.

Why, however, he'd chosen to broach this particular subject to her, right now, was anybody's guess. Had he sniffed the tension in the air, somehow suspected she and his dad had something to tell him? Although when that was gonna happen was also anybody's guess. Not that she couldn't understand why Aidan was still dragging his heels, but this particular pot of beans was getting heavier by the minute.

"Yeah," the boy said, his brow puckered as he concentrated on carving. "Mom said my birth mother was really nice and all, but she would've had a real hard time taking care of me, on account of she was really young and all alone and stuff. So she picked Mom and Dad to give me to."

Something in his voice put her on alert. Oh, Lord…what else had June told Robbie about her? Like, for instance, that his birth mother could've kept contact with him, but changed her mind when he was six months old? "Did—did your dad ever talk to you about it?"

"Uh-uh, just Mom. Mom said they'd been looking for a baby for a really long time, but that once they got me they understood why they'd had to wait."

Despite the ever-widening hole in her heart, Winnie

smiled. "It's true. They were very, very lucky to get you." She went back to her drawing, even though she could barely see what she was doing. "I bet you feel the same way."

When the child didn't respond, Winnie looked over to see his chin quivering. "Robbie—?"

"Mom *died.* How is that *lucky?*"

"Oh, honey…" Oh, *hell.* "Bad things happen to everybody at some time or other. Which doesn't make it hurt any less, I know. But the hurt can't take away from the good, either." She reached over to curl her fingers around his wrist, gratified when he didn't pull away. "I'm sure your mama loved you very, very much. Probably from the moment she laid eyes on you," she added over the stab of pain. "She still does, I'm sure. Wherever she is, I'll bet she's keeping an eye on you, wishing you the best."

Just like I do.

"I don't believe in heaven."

"That's okay, you don't have to."

"Dad says nobody's proved there's a heaven."

"Nobody's proven there isn't, either," Winnie said mildly. "Sometimes, it's about having faith."

"What's that mean?"

"Trusting in things you can't see or touch, but you feel in your heart. Like love. Even though you can't see or talk to your mama anymore, you can still remember her love. And nothing and nobody can take that away from you. Not ever."

Robbie looked skeptical, but he didn't argue. Instead he went back to his pumpkin. Only to suddenly say, a moment later, "Do you think Tess might give Julia away to somebody else?" and Winnie's head nearly snapped off her neck, she turned so fast.

"Why on earth would you think that?"

"Because she's all alone, too."

"Oh. Well, not in the same way that…that we were talking about before. Because Tess is married, even if her husband's in the army and too far away to come visit whenever he wants. And she's got Flo. And a job. And a place to live—"

"And she loves the baby too much to give her away, right?"

Her stomach all rubbery, Winnie got up and went to the sink for a drink of water, nearly tripping over Annabelle, who'd been asleep at her feet the whole time. She took a long swallow, then said, "Honey…giving a baby up for adoption doesn't necessarily mean a woman doesn't love the baby. In fact, often it's just the opposite, because a woman feels she wouldn't be able to give the baby everything it needs. Just like your mama told you, about…your birth mother? But sometimes single women do keep their babies. It just depends."

Robbie frowned. "On what?"

"Lots of things. Like whether or not you have the money and education to take care of a child. Not to mention the self-confidence."

"What's that mean?"

"Feeling good about yourself, that you can do whatever you have to do. Younger women, especially—like teenagers—sometimes just don't feel ready to be mothers."

The little boy seemed to think about this for a while, then said, "I bet if you had a baby, you'd never give away it away, huh?" and her heart exploded into a hundred million pieces.

Just as Aidan walked into the kitchen.

Winnie only met Aidan's gaze for a second, but that was still long enough for him to see the guilt screaming in her eyes. Not that he possessed Winnie's talent for "reading" people—nor did he lament that particular shortcoming: getting below the surface was not his thing—but with Winnie it was like having the open book shoved into your face.

Especially considering Robbie's hit-below-the-belt question.

"Robbie," he said, forcing his gaze to his son, "why don't you take Annabelle outside to play for a little while?"

"But I'm not finished my pumpkin!"

"You can finish up later. See? Annabelle's already at the door—" hearing her name, the dog had bounced to her feet, ready for action "—waiting for you to let her out."

When the door swooshed shut behind boy and dog, Winnie said, shakily, "We don't dare wait any longer, Aidan."

"So I gathered." He sighed. "But how on earth did the subject come up?"

"Who knows? Tess being here with the baby, maybe?" She frowned. "Did you know June had talked to him about me? Not by name, obviously. But the circumstances surrounding the adoption."

"No. When?"

"I don't know, he didn't say." She braced her palms on her thighs, her elbows jutting out as she glowered at her jack-o-lantern. "I had no idea this would be even harder than giving him up."

Aidan walked over to the kitchen window, ostensibly to check on things outside. In reality to get away from the pain in her eyes.

"I know what you're thinking," she said as she twisted around, her voice soft on his back, "that if I hadn't've come, none of this would be happening now. But I'm not so sure. With June gone…I suppose it makes perfect sense that he start thinking about his…birth mother."

He faced her, his emotions so tangled he couldn't sort one from the other. "You were going to say his *real* mother, weren't you?"

Her mouth pulled flat. "In my head, I know June's his real mother in every way that counts. Especially to Robbie. In my heart, though…" Skimming one fingertip over the ridges of the pumpkin she said, "You know the last thing I want is to upset Robbie. But after what he said…there's this really big part of me that wants a chance to explain that I didn't regift him like some Christmas present I got and didn't want.

"Oh, *God,* Aidan," she said, lifting tightly shut eyes to the beamed ceiling, and Aidan felt a rush of compassion so strong it made him dizzy. "This isn't what I meant to happen. Not at all. All I wanted was to get in, reassure myself that he was okay, get out. If I'd had any idea…" She opened her eyes, tears cresting on her lower lashes. "I never meant this to become such a huge mess."

You have no idea, Aidan thought, the ache to hold her nearly unbearable. "Except you didn't make this mess by yourself. I was just as responsible as you were. Possibly even more."

"And how do you figure that?"

His hands in his jacket pockets, he slipped into the chair across from her, catching her gaze. "Because when you offered to stay, I could have said no. And I didn't."

Several beats passed before she said, very quietly, "Why not?"

"Because I'm a selfish bastard," he said, pushing himself back to his feet. "Because, just for a little while, I wanted to pretend everything was normal. That *I* was normal. Except all I ended up doing was making a right fool of myself."

"Because you wanna feel normal?"

"Because for these last few days I forgot it was supposed to be all about Robbie." Aidan turned, letting his eyes caress what he refused to let his hand touch. "You can't tell me you weren't aware of what was happening between us yesterday, up on the mountain."

"So it wasn't my imagination?"

"That I let my guard down around you? That I *wanted* to let my guard down around you? That I wanted t'kiss you?" He shook his head. "No. You didn't imagine it."

"Then why didn't you?" she said, and he heard in her words a gift he didn't dare accept.

"Because I know normal's not something I'll ever be, or feel, again," he said, miserable. "And pretending's not good enough. Is it?"

Winnie sat so still, for so long, Aidan half wondered if she'd heard him. Until she sighed. "Damn. I'm not sure whether to be flattered or not." When he frowned, not understanding, she added, "If nothing else, you're sure not in the same place you were a week ago."

"And you think this is your doing?" When she shrugged, amusement toying with her mouth, he muttered, "Take it as you will, then."

She watched him for a moment, then stood and walked into the great room. Idly, she picked up one of the smaller *santos,* a rough-carved St. Michael, its bright colors softened from a hundred years of handling. "Do you pretend what you feel for Robbie?"

Aidan felt the jolt all the way through his body. "No!" he said, following her. "Of course not."

Winnie set the *santo* back down, then turned, her arms crossed. "Then let's get back on track and remember this isn't about what either of us feel. Or want. It's about a nine-year-old-boy who probably wants *normal* back more than anything in the world. And that's never again gonna include June, Aidan," she said, so gently he nearly recoiled. "Not in the same way. And if I could give Robbie a *tenth* of what June did—if nothing else, just to let him know I care—that would mean the world to me."

Her words pierced his heart. And, perhaps, the mist of denial he'd been living in for the past year.

Or at least the past week.

"We'll tell him after supper then, shall we?" he said, and Robbie said behind him, "Tell me what?"

* * *

Her heart knocking, Winnie vaguely mused about how it might've been nice to give her emotions a second to rally from this newest onslaught before getting slammed with yet another wave. But one look at Robbie's face wiped Aidan's *Nope, no hope on this front* expression right off the radar, if not her heart, where it had lodged like an enormous splinter.

They'd been so involved in their conversation they'd never noticed when Robbie and Annabelle came back in, or how long he'd been standing in the kitchen, listening to their conversation. Enough, though, she imagined, to figure out that he'd been the primary subject.

Lord, it was like watching a boulder teetering on the brink of a cliff and not being able to do a damn thing to stop it from going over.

"What're you talking about?" he said, inching into the great room, his hand clutched in Annabelle's ruff as his eyes darted between Winnie and Aidan.

Winnie remembered the whisperings in her grandmother's kitchen the night her parents died, when she'd crept downstairs to find out who'd been ringing the doorbell so late, the betrayal she'd felt when, after sending her back to bed, her grandmother kept the truth to herself for another three days.

After a quick glance at Aidan, who nodded, she looked back at Robbie. *Steady, girl,* she thought, then said, "Honey…you know how we were just talking about your birth mother?"

"Yeah…"

"That's…me."

"You?" Robbie said, his pale brows drawn together.

Winnie nodded, giving him time to absorb the news. Still frowning, he slowly squatted beside the dog, not even reacting when Annabelle decided the boy's face needed washing. Her heart about to pound out of her chest, Winnie's eyes shot again to Aidan, totally focused on his son.

"Laddie—?"

"You knew, huh?" he said, his head popping up, and the boulder teetered a little more.

"Robbie, I—"

"Why didn't you tell me?" the boy said, his words launched at Winnie as he shot to his feet, making the dog scramble out of the way. "When I came to see you at the Old House, why didn't you tell me then?"

"Because I asked her not to," Aidan said in an attempt to take the fire, but Robbie was having none of it.

"You're *not* my mom!" he yelled, tears bulging in his eyes. "My mom *died!* And you…you…" He backed clumsily away, bumping into the corner of the kitchen table. "I don't care what Mom said, you didn't *want* me, you *gave me away,* an'…an' you can't come back now and pretend everything's okay!"

"No, sugar, I'm not…" Heartsick, Winnie started toward him. "Of course I'm not trying to take your mom's place, I just thought—"

"You *lied* to me! You both lied to me! *No!*" he shrieked when Aidan tried to take him in his arms. *"Leave me alone!"* The instant Aidan let go, Robbie bolted toward the stairs, nearly knocking Flo over as she came up from the lower level.

"Hey! Watch it, buddy!" she said, this time dodging Aidan as he barged upstairs after the boy. Then she frowned at Winnie. *"Dios mío,"* she whispered, crossing herself. "You told him."

"We'd already made the decision," Winnie muttered as she stamped back into the kitchen, grabbing several paper towels off the rack to clean up the mess. "It was time, Flo," she said to the woman's horrified eyes. "I'd just hoped…" Her mouth clamped shut to keep the tears in, Winnie plopped the gunked up towels into the bowl full of pumpkin guts and carted them both over to the sink. "And I could really, really use some encouraging words right now, okay?"

From upstairs, Robbie wailed. "Man," Flo said, her eyes lifted. "I don' think I *ever* heard him cry like that."

"Not exactly what I had in mind."

"What do you wan' me to say? You come here uninvited, you get under everybody's skin—"

Winnie spun around. "And how's your wrist today, Flo?"

"I didn' *plan* on spraining my wrist—!"

"Neither did I! Lucky for you I was around, though. Right? *Right?*" she repeated when the older woman sniffed. "Still, if you hadn't…" She sighed. "I would've been long gone by now and Robbie would've forgotten about me soon enough. Dammit, Flo," Winnie said, blinking hard, "I *know* things got out of hand, but…but why the *hell* am I talking to *you* about this?"

"Where are you going?" Flo called behind Winnie as she started toward the stairs.

"Where do you think—?"

Winnie let out a yip when Flo's claws clamped around her arm, yanking her around. She glanced down, then back into the black eyes.

"I'm guessing your wrist is much better."

"It was up until a second ago. For godssake…don' you think you've caused enough heartache? Leave the boy alone," she said, more pleading than threatening. "Please. Leave them *both* alone."

Winnie wavered for barely a moment before easily extracting her arm from Flo's weakened grasp. "Soon," she said, and headed for the stairs.

"Robbie?"

Seated on the edge of Robbie's bed, his hand on the inconsolable child's back, Aidan twisted around at the sound of Winnie's voice, every muscle tensing with single-minded purpose—to protect his child.

"I d-don't want to talk to y-you!" came Robbie's muffled, jerky response.

"You don't have to," Winnie said softly, coming just far enough into the room to sit sideways on the chair in front of his desk. Her eyes swerved to Aidan's, determined. Defiant.

"One minute," she mouthed. After a moment, he nodded, once, then averted his gaze, knowing hearing her would be hard enough without having to watch her, too.

"Okay, Robbie," she said, "I know you're real mad at me right now. And I don't blame you. I messed up but good." When Aidan's head jerked around anyway, she cut him off with a raised hand. "The thing is, though…I guess I was trying to fix an earlier mess-up, even if I didn't completely realize it. Only sometimes when you try to do that, everything gets even more tangled."

Underneath his hand, Aidan felt Robbie still, his tears reduced to hiccupy sniffles.

"I know what you must be thinking, that if a mother loves her baby enough, she'd figure out a way to keep him, no matter what. But it really is a lot more complicated than that. Because if the baby's mama knows she can't do right by her child and keeps him anyway…that's not love, that's selfishness. See, sugar, sometimes, loving your baby isn't enough. Sometimes, you gotta make some real hard choices about what's best. Choices that hurt like nobody's business."

She cleared her throat, took a moment. "And now comes the hardest part of all, the part I really don't wanna tell you. But now that I know you, you deserve to know the whole truth. No more lies, okay?"

After a couple of seconds, Robbie nodded. Since Aidan knew Winnie couldn't see it, he nodded, as well, giving her the go-ahead.

"Okay, good," she said, then took another deep breath

before saying, "your mama and daddy and I had originally decided that I'd be a part of your life, even though they were going to raise you. Not a big part, but the plan was that we'd know each other, that we'd exchange letters from time to time, that maybe I'd even get to see you occasionally. Except…I couldn't go through with it. I thought I could, that I'd be okay with sharing a tiny piece of you…but the fact is, it hurt too much, honey. Your mama'd send me pictures of you, and not being able to feel you in my arms…"

She sat on her hands, her eyes fixed on her lap. "I couldn't handle it, baby. I just couldn't. So when you were about six months old, I told them to stop. And I know that makes me the biggest chicken on the face of the earth, but that's who I was then. I also discovered that my 'plan' didn't work worth beans. Because I don't think a day's gone by that I haven't thought about you. Wondered how you were doing, what you might look like.

"So," she said on a long breath, "fast forward to a couple weeks ago, and I get this crazy idea in my head that I had to see you, just once. That was all…just *see* you. And…well, you know what happened after that. Lord, it was like setting an itty-bitty snowball rolling down a mountain and by the time it reached the bottom it had turned into the size of a small planet, wipin' out everything in its path."

Pulling her hands out from under her thighs, she rubbed them over her legs, her eyes glued to Robbie, who still hadn't moved. Then she stood. "I feel like dirt, Robbie. Because I never, ever meant to hurt you. And I know I could never, ever be to you what your mama was. But I love you, you hear me? Whether you want me to love you or not. And I will treasure these days we had together for the rest of my life, even if we never speak to each other again."

After a brief pause, she turned to Aidan, her eyes saying, *Same goes for you,* before she walked out of the room.

Chapter Twelve

Winnie thought it very telling that when she tried to leave this time, fate stood aside with her hands lifted and just let her go. Of course, that might've had something to do with her taking off long before fate—or anybody else—was awake.

Since there seemed to be no sense in hanging around where she clearly wasn't wanted—or needed—she and Annabelle moved back down to the Old House right after her one-sided conversation with Robbie, where Winnie proceeded to drive herself crazy with the what-ifs. A dozen different scenarios had traipsed through her head, none of 'em ending any better than what had actually happened. If she hadn't've stayed…if she hadn't've come…if she hadn't've cut off communication with the Blacks all those years ago…if she hadn't've given up Robbie…if she hadn't've gotten pregnant to begin with…

"Every single thing you do has consequences, and don't you forget it," she said to Annabelle, keeping an eagle eye out for frosted roadkill as they sped east along I-40. Annabelle flicked her ears, just to be polite, but she didn't have much else to add to the conversation.

Winnie did wonder, however, as she poked Annabelle to hand her the last corner of her breakfast burrito, then licked her fingers, how human beings managed to get everything so balled up. Winnie herself being the grand champion, she thought with a smirk. Of course, there was Aidan—and would you look at that, she actually thought his name without falling apart—who clearly loved Robbie with all his heart and really, truly did want the best for him. But honestly, she thought as she zipped over the Texas border just as the sun inched over the horizon, getting by would be so much easier without all those sloppy emotions screwing up a person's reasoning ability.

In any case—she reached up to yank down the sun visor, down to twist on the radio, wincing when Willie Nelson's "You Were Always on My Mind" filled the cab—at least now she knew how things stood. She'd done what she set out to do, even if her little adventure had taken more turns than a twisty straw. And even if Robbie never wanted to see or talk to her again, in her heart she sincerely doubted he'd suffer forever from a relationship of less than a week's duration.

Just as she wouldn't, no matter how much that heart was hurting right now.

So. Time to head back home, get on with her real life. Figure out a thing or six. Like how to make that real life look more like her own instead of her grandmother's hand-me-down.

Blinking back tears, Winnie took a pull from her Big Gulp, swishing the ice-cold soda around her dry mouth even though it made her teeth hurt. At least that distracted her from the far bigger ache in the center of her chest. "For heaven's sake," she said aloud to the dog, who angled her head back to look at her, "who the hell falls in love in a *week?*"

Annabelle sighed and schlurped Winnie's cheek, then went back to roadkill watch, and Winnie returned to considering all the ways she'd made a fool of herself in such a short amount of time.

Miss Ida, she thought wryly, would have expected no less of her.

"What d'you mean, she's gone?"

"Jus' what I said, you don' understan' perfectly good English this morning?" Flo handed Aidan a piece of paper. "It don' say much, jus' that she's sorry an' that if she left anything behind, to send it to her at this address."

"I'm perfectly capable of readin' it m'self," Aidan snapped, glancing at the terse note before he stomped out of the house, folding the paper into quarters and stuffing it into his jeans' pocket as he strode to his truck. Considering how loathe she'd been to drive back in the dark before…

His stomach churning, he punched Winnie's number into his cell, irritated beyond belief when the call went to voice messaging. A few jostled minutes later he stood in front of the Old House, having no earthly idea why, or what he expected to find. But as he stood there, a sharp gust of wind blew open the unlocked front door, as if inviting him inside.

He found the bed stripped, the kitchen spotless, the refrigerator empty, as though she'd never been there. However, while he stood listening to the wind whining through the trees outside, as he had a thousand times before when he and June had lived there, he realized there was no trace of his wife left in the house, either.

Just an old, empty house, he thought, filled with nothing but the tattered, fragile cobwebs of memories.

And yet, stubbornly, because nothing irked him more than an unanswered phone, he tried Winnie again, this time texting her—"R u ok?"—barely registering Robbie's bicycle clattering onto the porch before he heard the lad's, "Dad? What're you doing here?" behind him.

"Winnie's gone," Aidan said, turning.

"I know," Robbie said, coming inside. "Flo told me."

His gaze darted around, almost as though he was looking for something. Or someone. "She's not here," he said quietly.

"Of course not, I just told you Winnie'd left."

"What?" The boy's eyes shot to his. "I didn't mean…" Frowning, he shook his head. "Never mind." Then his chin came up—Winnie's chin—defiance not quite blotting out the pain. A pain Aidan knew was his fault as well as Winnie's. "I'm still mad at you, you know."

"I'm sure you are. I'm none too pleased with myself at the moment."

"Lying stinks," Robbie said, then added, "But we don't need Winnie, huh?"

And that's the truth of it, isn't it? Who needed the aggravation, the stirred-up emotions? Who needed some *stranger* making them think about things they didn't want to think about, things they were just as happy not to feel? His smile tight, Aidan drew his son close to his side.

"No, laddie, we certainly do not," he said, refusing to believe the words that felt as empty as the house.

Sometime in the middle of the morning, Winnie banged through the diner's door, nearly tripping over Annabelle as she made straight for the pastry tower, dumping her duffel and nagging a piece of lemon meringue pie.

"I'm back," she said to Elektra, who was standing behind the register with a "what the hell?" look on her face.

"So I noticed. Since I didn't go blind in your absence."

A snort tossed in E's direction, Winnie waved to Andy, the cook, when he yelled, "Hey, Winnie," from the kitchen, over the familiar clunks and clatters as he geared up for the lunch "rush." The day waitresses, who started at six, were on break. Nothing much doing this time of day, except for travelers coming in to pay for gas, use the john, grab chips and sodas and leave. "Everything okay?" Winnie said, plunking her butt onto the stool closest to E, her mouth full of tart lemon filling and sweet, airy meringue.

"Depends on what you mean by everything." Elektra leaned over to give Annabelle some love, straightening up again with a grunt. "Place is still here, I'm still alive, no tornadoes came through or anything."

"I see winning the lottery hasn't changed you."

"That's probably because it ain't sunk in yet. When they give me the check, then I'll believe it. How come you didn't let me know you were on your way? And did you forget how to use a fork during your travels?"

"Don't need one," Winnie mumbled, shoving the next bite into her mouth, glowering at the accordion file in E's out-stretched hand, filled with the week's receipts. Winnie wiped her sticky fingers on her jeans, then reluctantly pawed through the file, noting that they'd had a good week and this realiza-tion produced not a shred of excitement. Or even satisfaction.

She definitely had the *motive* to move on. Now all she needed was the kick in the butt to actually do it.

"And you can stop gawking anytime," she said, wiping a smudge of lemon filling off the corner of one receipt.

"Soon as you tell me what happened, I'll stop gawking."

Winnie stuffed the receipts back into the file, thinking, *So where's an Option C when you need one?* "What happened was, I learned several things about myself, topping the list being that I think my impulsive streak and I have parted company for good. Two, that horseback riding when you haven't been for fifteen years is probably not a good idea. Three..." On a sigh, she glanced around the diner. "That I'm sellin' the diner."

E's eyebrows shot up. "And when did you decide this?"

"About thirty seconds before I walked through that door."

"So much for parting company with your impulsive streak."

Winnie reached over to wrap her hand around E's. "I promise, I won't sell to anybody who won't keep you on. And pay you what you're worth, which Miss Ida sure as hell never did. But if I stay here…I'll end up just like her. And that, honeychile, ain't gonna happen. I may have been an eejit about other things, but I'm not gonna be about this."

Elektra frowned. "Egypt?"

"Not Egypt. Eejit. Idiot in Irish."

"I see. Nice to see your self-esteem issues made the trip there and back intact."

"Oh, hell, E, I tossed those out years ago. Right about the time I realized I was not responsible for my grandmother's misery. However," she said, stuffing the remainder of the pie into her mouth, "even smart, confident people do dumb things now and again." She swallowed. "Like falling in love with people they shouldn't, for example."

E's face went all soft and sympathetic. "Oh, honey… the boy?"

"Yeah, I guess I kinda left my heart out there with Robbie. Even if he didn't want it."

"What do you mean, he didn't want it?"

Dry-eyed, Winnie gave her the abridged version of what had transpired the previous night. When she was done, Elektra said, "So you ran like a scared rabbit instead of staying put until the child came around." When Winnie squawked, she added, "Honey, it takes a *lot* for a kid to hate somebody. Most likely he's just mad. And prob'ly confused. He'll also get over it. Although you'll never know, will you, being as you're here and he's there? You're right—that *was* dumb. A whole lot dumber than you goin' out there to begin with."

"Yeah, good thing I don't have those self-esteem issues anymore."

"Like you said, smart people can do dumb things. You're one of the smartest gals I know. But that was, without a doubt, the most boneheaded stunt you've ever pulled."

"And you haven't even heard the best part. Because I didn't…" She took a breath, hardly believing the words about to come out of her mouth. "Because I didn't just fall in love with my kid."

"Oh, hell," Elektra said after *maybe* a half second. "You didn't."

"Yep. Head over heels," Winnie said, reaching for another piece of pie. Cherry, this time.

E slapped her hand. "Honey, you seriously need to redefine *'parting company.'*"

"I didn't say I *acted* on the impulse. And give me the pie, dammit."

"You don't need no more pie, your butt's not as skinny as it used to be, in case you hadn't noticed."

"And isn't that like the pot calling the kettle…round."

"Baby, I was born with this butt, I could eat nothin' but lettuce and I'd still look like this. Only I'd be mean as hell 'cause I'd be hungry all the damn time."

"Yeah, well…" Winnie stood on the rung of the stool to grab the pie out of E's hand. "Since it's been years since anybody other than Annabelle's seen me naked," she said, plunking back onto the stool, "I'll take my chances."

"Years…? Oh. So…you didn't…?"

"I said I didn't act on it, didn't I? Not that there was exactly loads of opportunity. But Funland was definitely ready for its grand reopening." As E went on about people managing to find ways to have sex if they want it bad enough, Winnie pulled out her cell phone and scrolled to a photo she'd taken of Aidan and Robbie when they'd gone riding. Still chewing, she held up the phone.

"Damn," E said a good five seconds later.

"Yep," Winnie said, slapping shut the phone and dumping it on the counter in front of her.

"So I take it this was one-sided?"

"What it was, was pointless. And dumb."

"You already said that."

"It bears repeating—"

Her phone buzzed, shimmying on the counter.

"You gonna get that?" Elektra said, eying the thing like she couldn't decide whether to take the fly swatter to it or what.

"Nope," Winnie said, shoveling in another bite of pie. "Since I know who it is— Hey! Give that back!"

"Five-oh-five?" E said, scooting away from Winnie with remarkable agility for a woman of her prodigious proportions. "Ain't that New Mexico? You want me to answer it?"

"No!" Winnie bellowed as she finally reached E and snatched the phone out of her hand. Elektra's eyes narrowed.

"Tell me you didn't just up and leave without saying nothin'?"

"I…decided to get an early start. I didn't want to wake anybody."

Now the eyes were little more than slits. "You know, I'm thinking you're like the Cowardly Lion, the Tin Man and the Scarecrow, all rolled up into one sorry-assed young woman. Only thing is, you were supposed to *find* all that stuff while you were on your little adventure, not lose it!"

"E, I—"

"I don't want to hear it, I truly don't. All that rebellin' you did when you were a teenager, all those times you'd deliberately get up Miss Ida's nose…what happened to that girl, huh? Where'd she go?"

"She grew up."

"Not from where I'm sitting, she didn't," E said, turning to smile for the young couple who just walked in.

Now thoroughly disgruntled, Winnie went around the counter, sure she'd find...yep, there they were, a half-dozen cinnamon rolls left from breakfast. She plunked one on her cherry-smeared plate, licking the gooey icing from her fingers. Annabelle whined up at her.

"It won't last the day, anyway," Winnie said, then sighed, wondering if she would.

Since one of the girls called in sick for lunch, and another was an hour late reporting for the dinner shift, it was nearly seven by the time Winnie finally got back to her—Ida's—house. Which is when she finally realized not answering Aidan's calls was silly and childish. And, she supposed, unfair. So, feeling marginally unwell, she curled up on her grandmother's puke-green, plastic-wrapped brocade sofa and called him.

"Where the bloody *hell* have you been?" he barked without saying hello. "I've texted you, left I don't know how many voice messages—"

"I was driving, I couldn't answer my cell. And then I had to fill in for two MIA waitresses—"

"You left in the middle of the damn night, before I even had a chance to explain—"

"There's nothing *to* explain! And anyway, I couldn't sleep." She stopped to control her voice. "Dammit, Aidan," she said softly, looking out her window, "for a week, I've been brave in ways I never knew I could be. Maybe in the larger scheme of things my brave isn't a whole lot, but it's all I've got. And apparently it only comes in small doses. Well, I used up my allotment for the week. And I had to get out of Tierra Rosa before—" *I lost it completely* "—before things got worse. Robbie's furious with me—"

"Not just with you, with both of us."

"Yeah, I suppose he is. With good reason. I should've never come."

"No, I shouldn't've been so afraid of the truth. I can't help wondering if things would've blown up the way they had if I'd been honest from the beginning." He paused. "If I hadn't put my own issues onto the lad."

Tears welled in her eyes. "How about we agree we both screwed up and leave it at that?"

"Fair enough. Ah, Winnie," he blew out, "I know we— I—handled it badly, but after the dust settles, I'm sure Robbie'll want to see you again."

"That's a lot of dust to settle. And even if he did…maybe that's not such a good idea."

"Why not? He's your *son,* for God's sake!"

"No, he's *your* son! Yours and June's! I'm just—"

"Hurt. And not only about Robbie."

"If I am," she said after a moment, "the wounds are entirely self-inflicted. There were more reasons than I can count why I shouldn't have let my feelings get out of hand. For either of you. But I did."

"I'm so sorry—"

"Why? Why should *you* be sorry? I was the one who got it into my head to go looking for my son, wedging myself into your lives—"

"There were two of us in it, Winnie. Which you damn well know."

"Up to a point, yeah, I suppose that's true. But I passed that point. Saw the flashing Do Not Enter signs and zoomed right on past them, anyway. And the thing is, I completely understand, Aidan, I really do. I met June, remember? And she's like everywhere on that mountain, you can just *feel* her, like the love she had for you and Robbie never left. So of *course* you're still in love with her, how could you not be? And maybe it was inevitable that I fall in love with Robbie, but falling in love with *you* was definitely not part of the deal!"

Silence stretched between them until Aidan said, "You remember Johnny Griego? From the horse farm?"

"Of course—"

"He and Thea—from Garcia's—have been an item for some time."

She frowned. "*That's* why he looked familiar—I saw them together that morning, when we had breakfast. Only neither of them looked too happy about things. Especially Thea."

"I suppose not, considering. Flo considers it her bounden duty to keep me in the loop about the village. Whether I want to be or not," he sighed. "Word is that Johnny's never completely got over his ex-wife, even though they've been divorced for years. At least, not enough to fully commit to Thea. But he's kept her dangling, holding out that carrot of hope, for years. D'you see?"

"Um…not really."

"I don't want to be like that. Stringin' you along, giving you false hope. Because doing anything by half isn't my way, and never has been. God knows I'm attracted to you, and care about you, but it's as if…as if everything's in place, but the alternator's missin'."

She sputtered a sniffly little laugh. "So the engine won't start. I got it. Although sounds to me like you better stick to painting, 'cause your way with words needs some serious fine tuning."

He laughed, too, then said softly, "You're grand, Winnie. Insane, but grand. Far too grand for the sorry likes of me. At first I thought I was resisting because I couldn't bear the thought of goin' through that kind of pain again. And maybe that's still part of it, I don't know. But I do know…I'm not keen on hurting anyone else, either." He paused. "Especially if that someone is you."

After he'd hung up and Winnie lay curled on her side on her bed, tears soaking into the mattress and Annabelle worriedly whining and nudging—*I fix it? Make it better?*—it occurred to her that she'd take some eejit leaving a snake in her front seat over this, any old day.

Some time later, her landline rang, jarring her out of a heavy sleep. She grabbed the portable out off her night-stand, muttering a groggy, "'Lo?" into it.

"I wanna buy the diner."

"E?" Winnie sat up, realizing it was pitch dark. "What—?"

"With my winnings. That's what I want to do with them. This way I don't have to worry about somebody else paying me a salary, 'cause I can damn well set my own. And I've already talked it over with Andy and the girls, and they're all on board. I know it's not quite enough, but if it's okay with you, I could maybe pay off the balance of the asking price over time from the profits…?"

When the pause had dragged on a bit, Winnie realized E was waiting on an answer. "Oh! Ohmigod, E! Okay?" She laughed. "Honey, that's the best damn idea anybody's had around here in a dog's age!"

"So…you think we could go on over to the lawyer's tomorrow and get the ball rolling?"

"Soon as they open the doors," she said, grinning.

She hung up. Annabelle nosed her knee, either because she was dying of curiosity about the call or she had to wee. "E's gonna buy the diner, girl," Winnie said, pushing herself up to go let the dog out back. Then, yawning, she stood on the back porch with her arms wrapped around herself, looking up into the clear, star-studded Texas sky. And it finally hit, that soon there'd be nothing to keep her in Skyview. That her life was finally and completely and totally hers, to do with as she pleased.

That E's winning that money and offering to buy the diner was nothing but a big old fat sign—aka the kick in the butt she was looking for—that it was time to move on.

"And that's definitely something to be joyful about,

isn't it?" she said to Annabelle when the dog came back up onto the porch, grinning. "And I didn't even have to wait until morning…."

Her chin wobbled a bit, but only for a moment.

Because those big-girl panties were fitting better and better every day.

Chapter Thirteen

Hands crammed into his back pockets, Aidan glowered at the trio of landscapes lined up against the far wall of the studio, luminous in the clear early November light, as the most recent round of heated words between him and Flo whirled inside his head like a dust devil.

Like many artists, he often revisited his subjects. Landscapes in particular, always changing at the whim of the light, the weather, the season. In Aidan's case, however, the three paintings in front of him had been far more shaped by his moods than any external factor. The gauzy, snow-glittered sunrise painted before June's illness epitomized contentment and promise; the second one, a sunset past its peak done a month or so after her death, was static, dull, lifeless—the color leached from the sky, the mountains morose and mauve instead of a vibrant watermelon.

Then there was the one of the churning, charcoal-skied

storm encroaching on the blazing sunset. The one Winnie'd dubbed "Angry Sex."

Massaging his temple, Aidan sagged back onto a step-stool, eyeing the canvas. The day Winnie left, if Flo had said "It's just as well she's gone" once, she'd said it a hundred times. This past week, however, she'd been constantly on about how much grumpier Aidan was now than before Winnie'd come. And his stubborn insistence that he was fine only brought return fire about how "fine" meant more than simply breathing in and out every day. "The chick made you *laugh*, boss," she'd said. "Now it's like somebody died all over again."

Bloody cheek.

And although he might be able to ignore his house-keeper—the great effort that took notwithstanding—only an eejit would miss what these paintings were saying, that a man could tell himself, tell the world, he was done with letting himself feel till the cows came home, but that wouldn't keep the feelings from coming.

Like the one squeezing the life out of him right now, that he'd been unsuccessfully trying to ignore from the moment he realized Winnie was gone, that he missed her with an intensity that bordered on panic. Not more than he'd missed his wife, perhaps, but close enough to make him realize…

To make him realize that the missing was only going to get worse, because Winnie was *alive*, dammit, and *had* made him laugh, made him feel alive again himself, made him realize that maybe he really didn't want to bloody well sit up on his mountain for the rest of his days, with nothing but the chickens and his work and a smart-mouthed house-keeper to keep him company. Because Robbie would one day go out into the world to claim his own life, leaving his poor old da behind to solace himself with what used to be.

And wasn't that a load of bollocks?

Aidan got up to move closer to the painting, the one brimming with fire and anger and passion and fear and frustration, and he shut his eyes and tilted his head back, seeing Winnie's face, and he let out a low moan, thinking that not having the courage to look at a subject—like, for instance, love and home and family—from a different angle, at a different season, is a sure way to miss all those glorious new colors—

"Dad?"

There is that, Aidan thought, turning, seeing Winnie again, this time in his son—*her* son—in his eyes and his hair and the do-or-die set to the boy's chin. Because as long as Robbie still felt the way he did about what had happened, whatever conclusions Aidan might have reached about his own feelings for Winnie were moot.

Under Flo's instruction, two nights ago they'd even held a makeshift Day of the Dead ceremony for June, setting up an altar of sorts in the family room with candles and cheerful, gaily dressed skeletons, a plate of cheese enchiladas—June's favorite food—and every photograph they could find of her. Then he and Robbie had dutifully sung her favorite songs, and sifted through more memories than he'd realized he even had, celebrating her life—their lives together—rather than mourning her death.

Certainly Aidan hadn't done it for himself, but for the lad, hoping the ceremony might at least pierce the cloud that had settled again in the boys' eyes. But no such luck. To Aidan's surprise, however, the ache in his own heart *had* begun to ease, as though June had actually been present, laughing right along with them.

But there were moments when he'd heard Winnie's laughter, too, seen her wide grin, felt her give him a thumbs-up. Felt her love, so generously given with little heed to the risks. In reading up on the traditions behind the ceremony, Aidan had run across the sentiment that the only true way to celebrate death is to live with courage…something he surely hadn't been doing.

But, as always, this wasn't only about him.

"You promised we could go riding today!" Robbie now said. "Only if we don't go *right now* it'll be too late!" Then the squeezing started up all over again, and Aidan heard June saying, *Do it for him, babe.*

For me.

For yourself.

For the first time in his life, he began to understand why people asked for signs.

After Winnie'd gone, Robbie had tried as hard as he could to keep the mad feeling alive inside him, because the mad burned up the hurt. And it had worked, sorta, for a little while, until he finally realized he just felt more mixed up than anything. Especially after the Day of the Dead ceremony him and Dad'd held for Mom a couple days ago, when it felt like he was being told to let go of something he wasn't ready to let go of yet.

Only then he realized it was being taken away from him anyway, whether he was ready or not. And this morning he woke up and thought, *Now.* Just like that. That it was time to stop thinking about the sad stuff so much. Time to talk to Dad about…about Mom.

When they got to the farm, he'd been totally shocked when Johnny and Dad decided Robbie's legs were long enough to ride Maggie instead of Patches. And at first it was kinda scary, sitting up so high, but he got used to it pretty quick, especially since it felt pretty cool to ride beside Dad and be able to look him right in the eye when they talked. Dad had pretty much let Robbie say whatever he wanted without interrupting, even when he could hardly get the words out the way they sounded in his head.

"At first I thought I was just mad at Winnie and you,"

Robbie said, watching Maggie's head bob up and down as the horses walked. "For not telling me, mostly." Maggie started to speed up; Robbie gently tugged the reins to slow her down, feeling a little tickle of warmth when she did. "I could tell you and Winnie were keeping something from me. I just didn't know what. Just like I knew something was wrong with Mom, too, before you told me she was sick."

He could feel Dad's frown. "You did?" When Robbie nodded, looking straight ahead, Dad blew out a breath. "I'm sorry, laddie, I had no idea." He was a quiet for a moment, then said, "Is that why you didn't feel you could talk to me about your mother?"

Robbie hadn't really figured that part of things out, but as soon as Dad said it, it made total sense. "Maybe."

Dad sighed again, then said, "We really bollixed that up, didn't we? But why didn't you say something? About Mom, I mean."

"I guess because…I figured if it was something you didn't want to tell me, it was pretty bad." For a moment, his chin got all shaky. "But it was a lot scarier wondering what was wrong but not knowing. Like a bad dream where you can't actually see the monster, but you can feel him, y'know? So you're like holding your breath the whole time, w-wondering when he's gonna jump out at you."

Dad took off his cowboy hat to run his hand through his hair, then put the hat back on. "Ah, Robbie…sometimes grown-ups forget to give their kids credit for being a lot more on the ball than they think." Robbie looked over the same time Dad looked at him, catching his sorta smile. "I just hope one day you understand Mom and I kept the truth from you because we didn't want you to worry. Especially since we hoped…" He sighed. "We'd both hoped Mom would get better. But I should've also trusted your ability to handle the truth about Winnie. I'd no right to take out my anger at her on you."

Robbie frowned. "Why were you mad?"

"That she'd shown up with no warning, mostly. That...that she'd changed her mind about keeping contact with you so long ago. I was afraid she'd hurt you all over again. Especially since I knew you were still hurtin' about Mom...you want to stop for a bit, give your legs a chance to adjust?"

"Sure."

They dismounted and tethered their horses to the lower branches of a piñon, then walked over to a look-out with a view of the mesas to the south. "You know what really sucks?" Robbie said. "Now that I know who Winnie is, it ruins *everything*."

He stumbled a little when Dad put an arm around his shoulders and tugged him to his side. "And why's that?" he said gently.

"I don't know. It just does."

Dad stayed quiet for a while, until he finally said, "Because y'think she gave you away, you mean?" When Robbie nodded, his eyes all stingy, Dad said, "I don't suppose you remember what she said to you, the night she left?"

"It doesn't change anything," Robbie said, still trying to hold on to the mad. Except it was like his fingers were slipping, like when he was too little to go all the way across the monkey bars at school and he'd fall off.

"D'you know how many couples Winnie interviewed before she decided to let Mom and me have you?" Dad said, his voice real quiet over Robbie's head. "More than a dozen. So y'see, she was very, very particular about who she'd let raise her precious little boy. That's not the act of someone who doesn't care, Robbie. Even if she couldn't *take* care of you. And I'm afraid I'm going to have to play the grown-up card and ask you to trust me—and Winnie—on that. Because I doubt I can explain it so it makes sense to you."

Robbie ducked out from underneath Dad's arm and walked back to stroke Maggie's soft nose. Whuffling, the horse bent her head, and something about her big, brown eyes…

The horse nodded, then carefully nibbled Robbie's hair. "I feel like…like there's too many thoughts inside my head, and they're all crashing into each other."

Behind him, Dad chuckled. "Tell me about it."

Robbie looked up. "You, too?"

"Oh, yeah. Big-time."

Robbie looked back at the horse. "I guess I said some really mean stuff. 'Specially about how I thought Winnie was trying to take Mom's place."

"Everybody says things in the heat of the moment they come to regret. I doubt Winnie holds it against you."

"But she left."

"I don't think she felt she had any choice." A moment passed before Dad added, "Neither one of us gave her much of a reason to stay, did we?"

Robbie thought about that for a while, then said, "I really miss her."

"You're not the only one," Dad said, patting Maggie's neck and frowning, and Robbie thought maybe Dad didn't mean it the same way Robbie did.

"But…I guess part of the reason I'm so mixed up is because Winnie was beginning to feel like more than a friend, she was beginning to feel like a mom. And I was feeling really bad about that. Especially since you didn't like her very much."

Dad frowned at him, surprised. "What makes you think I didn't like her?"

"Okay, maybe you didn't *hate* her or anything. But every time you'd get close to her, like on accident or something? You'd back up, like you didn't want to touch her."

"Oh," Dad said, looking away, his cheeks all dark, like he'd gotten sunburned. "Well, that's because…I didn't want to invade her personal space."

"Huh?" Robbie said, but Dad just kinda shrugged, like he couldn't explain himself any better. So Robbie said, "Anyway, so there I was, liking Winnie more than I thought I should, only I wasn't sure if that was okay or not."

Dad cleared his throat. "Yeah. It's okay."

"You don't think Mom would mind?"

"Do you think she would?"

Robbie thought about it, then shook his head. "No. Actually, I think she'd like Winnie."

"She did like Winnie," Dad said. "When they met. Right before you were born."

"Good," Robbie said. "Because…because why can't I love Winnie and still love Mom? And anyway, it's not like sending Winnie away's gonna bring Mom back."

Dad reached over to mess with Robbie's hair. "Smart lad," he said in a funny voice, and Robbie looked up to see Dad staring into the distance with a strange expression on his face.

"Don't get me wrong," Robbie said, feeling brave, "I'm still mad as *heck* that nobody told me the truth. And it's not like Winnie's suddenly my mom or anything. *Mom's* my mom, okay? But if I liked Winnie before I found out she was my mother…" He looked away, shaking his head. "Why would I feel any different after?"

They stood there for a long time, watching a bunch of dead leaves blowing around, before Dad said, "Do you actually think we sent her away?"

"It sure feels like that."

Dad nudged Robbie's arm with his, making Robbie look up at him. "So what d'you think we should do?"

"I dunno. Maybe…call her or something? Tell her we're sorry?"

"Actually," Dad said, patting the horse, "I was thinking more along the lines of…" Smiling, he looked back at Robbie. "A trip to Texas?"

Robbie thought that sounded like a *grand* idea, as Dad

would say. Then a breeze blew across his cheek, feeling an awful lot like...

Like a goodbye kiss.

"I'll give you fifty bucks for the whole shebang," Bessie Jenkins said, beady little eyes clamped on the motley collection of china and glassware scattered across the dining table that Winnie's grandmother had hung on to like Jesus Himself would ask for them if and when he made a reappearance. By the gleam in those beady eyes, Winnie surmised Bessie—who made her living selling other people's junk at the flea market—had in all likelihood spotted a treasure in the detritus. Ask Winnie if she cared.

"Done," she said. "But you gotta take it with you, I promised Inez Montoya whatever I didn't sell by four she could have for the church thrift shop."

Bessie turned shocked eyes nearly the same vomit color as the shag wall-to-wall to Winnie, although whether because Winnie'd set a deadline or because she'd cut a deal with the Catholics, she couldn't say. "Why four?"

"Because I'm headed for Amarillo tonight."

This announcement apparently boosted the shock factor considerably, because now Bessie's eyes looked like they might ignite. "Amarillo?" the older woman said, as though Winnie had said she was moving to China instead of fifty miles down the interstate. "Why on earth—?"

"You need a box? I've got plenty in the garage."

Winnie took Bessie's weak nod as permission to duck outside. Annabelle rushed her, tennis ball in mouth. *People gone? I come back inside now?* "Not yet, baby," Winnie said, the cool air soothing her overheated skin as she crossed the small, brown-grassed yard with its single, pathetic little elm tree to get to the detached garage in back.

The crowds had thinned considerably since this morning—as had, thank God, a good portion of the sixties-era furnishings that Winnie doubted had looked much better new. Some couple had even given her a hundred bucks for the laminated sofa and matching armchair, bless their hearts. But honestly, Winnie had had no idea there were that many people within a hundred-mile radius, let alone how on earth they'd found her grandmother's house. Yes, it was in the middle of town, but that's not saying much when "town" is only ten blocks long.

A town she'd no longer call home after tonight.

As she rummaged in the frigid garage for boxes and newspapers, she tried to wrap her head around the fact that she was actually *leaving*. But once she and Elektra got all the paperwork sorted out—and Winnie had that first, glorious check in her hot little hands—she'd thought…*why stay?*

Why, indeed? She could crash with E's daughter and husband until she found a place of her own, she had enough money to live on until she found a job, and most any city you could name needed teachers. And if she threw herself wholeheartedly into starting a new life, in a new place, with fresh goals, maybe, just maybe, she'd eventually forget about all those things she couldn't stop thinking about.

Although she wasn't counting on it.

Boxes and papers dangling awkwardly from her person, Winnie started back across the yard, muttering curses when Annabelle took advantage of Winnie's full arms to wriggle past her through the back door.

"Annabelle!" she yelled, too late.

"Annabelle!" a child shrieked. Too familiar.

"Woof!" Annabelle woofed, and the child laughed, and Winnie stumbled into the living room, boxes and papers flying, her heart thundering, to see Robbie and the dog all tangled up and laughing on the floor. Okay, so maybe Annabelle wasn't really laughing, she wasn't going ha-ha-ha, but Winnie knew her dog, and her dog was *laughing*.

As opposed to the glowering Irish cowboy standing ten

feet in front of her, sucking all the air out of the room. Or maybe just her lungs.

"And just where the hell d'you think you're going?" he said, voice low, jaw rigid, gaze intense, and Bessie let out a little squeak.

Winnie, however, burst into tears.

Not exactly the reaction I'd hoped for, Aidan thought as Winnie ran from the room.

"Don't anybody move," he said, although he wasn't sure why, before taking off after her. He followed the series of open doors left in her wake until he found her, sobbing, out in what could only be described as the ugliest garden on God's green earth. Yes, even taking into consideration that it was November. It was, he thought, the garden of someone to whom nurturing was a completely alien concept. The thought of Winnie—bright, funny Winnie— forced to spend so much of her childhood here...

"Winnie," he breathed, crossing to take her in his arms, holding fast when she struggled to escape, kissing her hair, much as he had with Robbie when he'd get into a crying jag as a toddler.

"I'm sorry," he murmured when she finally relaxed. After a fashion. "I didn't mean to bark. But I stopped at the diner first and Elektra said I'd be lucky if you hadn't left already, and I panicked. That I was too late. That I'd lost you."

"That you'd...?" she said, watery eyes meeting his, but that's as far as she got before Aidan took her tear-tracked face in his hands and kissed the bejaysus out of her. Until she jerked away, frowning, shaking her head—

"Winnie?" he heard Robbie say behind them, and Winnie hurriedly scrubbed at her splotched cheeks, forcing a smile as Robbie pounded across the yard, the dog right beside him, to launch himself at her.

"I'm sorry, Winnie!" he said, his words muffled as he

buried his face in her sweatshirt. "I'm sorry I hurt your feelings!"

"Oh, Robbie," she said, kneeling, sniffling, stroking his hair off his face over and over. "You didn't hurt me, I hurt *you.* I didn't mean to, honestly, I probably shouldn't've tried to see you without clearing it with your dad first—"

"No, I'm glad you came," the boy said, suddenly an adult trapped in a child's body, and Aidan's heart swelled with pride and love, even as he could see Robbie's face morph through a dozen expressions as he desperately tried to sort out his thoughts. Finally he sniffed, wiped his nose on his sleeve, and simply repeated, "I'm *glad* you came. I swear."

"And so am I," Aidan said, in a voice he barely recognized as his own, and Winnie's red-rimmed eyes met his. And in them he saw hope. Fear. Disbelief. Maybe a little embarrassment.

She looked back at Robbie. "Then…I'm glad I came, too," she said, her smile all trembly before she yanked her son into her arms and held him tight, her eyes shut. "I love you, Robbie," she whispered fiercely. "No matter what you think of me, no matter what happens—" she released him, only to clasp his shoulders "—I love you. I always will." She ducked slightly to look into his eyes. "And I always have. Do you believe me?"

"I'm working on it," he said, and she laughed.

"Fair enough," she said, then again lifted questioning eyes to Aidan, and he thought, *There's half the battle won, at least.*

Winning the second half, however…

"So," Aidan said, "you were simply going to chuck it all and start over?"

Seated in the back of her truck, her legs dangling over the let-down tailgate, Winnie shrugged, trying to appear far more collected than she felt. Trying not to breathe in Aidan's scent—no mean feat since he was sitting less than a foot away. Resisting the temptation to skootch close enough for their thighs to touch. Because she knew, the minute she felt him or breathed him in or even really looked at him…she was lost.

Not an option for someone who'd just found herself.

Boy and dog left behind with E, it was just the two of them, parked in the middle of an abandoned field with nothing but the occasional distant coyote yip for company. "That was the plan, yep," Winnie said, zipping up her hoodie against the breeze. "The house is basically in good shape, the Realtor said it just needs a paint job and new carpet before she puts it on the market, the contractor's coming tomorrow after I'm gone."

"Do you have a buyer?"

Ignoring the not-so-thinly veiled *Are you nuts?* in his voice, Winnie said, "The house is bound to be perfect for someone, just not me."

"Still. Rather an impulsive move, don'cha think?"

She'd already told him about E's winning the lottery, the weirdness of her using Miss Ida's birthdate, how even if E defaulted the business would simply revert to Winnie, so it was a win-win situation for her. But she knew E wouldn't default, that this part of her life was well and truly over.

"Considering I've been planning my escape for nearly twenty years…not really. I'll miss E, of course—if it hadn't've been for her I would've lost my mind years ago—but I won't miss any of the rest of it."

Aidan made a move on her hand; she pulled away. He pointed out that she hadn't resisted when he'd taken her in his arms before; she pointed out that, actually, she had but he wouldn't take no for an answer.

If he'd been about to say something else, he changed his mind. Instead, he leaned back on his elbow in the truck bed, propping his wrist on his pulled-up knee. In front of them, the setting sun bled spectacularly into the horizon.

"Skyview's certainly an appropriate name. I should come back some day to paint this," he said, and she thought, *Then you'll have to do it without me.*

"Thought you'd like it," Winnie muttered, her heart breaking.

Aidan leaned forward to sweep her hair off her shoulder. "I've caught you off guard, and you're angry," he said softly, and her heart broke a little more.

"I'm not angry, I'm confused." She finally turned to him, seeing in those sweet, green eyes everything she'd ever wished for, even if she hadn't fully known it. Which was exactly what made him so dangerous. "I don't know what you want. Why you're here."

He curled his spine to sit upright again, a small smile playing around his mouth. "I certainly didn't come for the sky, as grand as it is. Or even to bring Robbie." The smile grew. "Which I'm sure you know. And now that I'm here…what I want, is for you to consider moving a bit farther west than Amarillo."

Winnie's heart started beating so hard she could hear it underneath her skull. "You're askin' me to come back with you to Tierra Rosa?"

"That was the plan, yep," he said, echoing her. Teasing. Except Winnie was not in the mood to be teased.

Her eyes burning, she looked back at the setting sun, now barely a ridge of fire at the edge of the earth. "A couple weeks ago you said—"

"That was then."

"And you expect me to believe you've done a complete one-eighty in that short amount of time?" She shook her head. "You're askin' a whole lot, Aidan. You're asking me to—"

"I'm asking you to believe me when I say that every time I look at the lad, I see you. Hear you. He's so much like you, Winnie. Stubborn and funny and bright as a new penny. Especially the stubborn thing. God, how that used to drive his mother and me nuts—"

Winnie turned in time to catch the flush of embarrassment. "It's okay," she said on a rush of air, looking away again. "June was his mother. And I'd never expect him, or you, to think about it any other way."

"Winnie. Winnie, look at me. Please." Against her better judgment, she did, falling so deep into those eyes she knew she'd never find her way out again. "I found the alternator," he said, and she laughed in spite of…everything. He took advantage of the moment to claim her hand, tucking it against his chest. "It's your heart I'm asking for, Winnie. And I *promise* you, I'll take very good care of it."

Her throat caught. "And you know you already have it," she whispered.

"Then I'm asking for your soul," he said, pressing his lips to her fingers, his eyes never leaving hers. The corners of his mouth lifted. "Your body, if you're willing. And anything else you feel like sharing."

"And…in return?"

His eyes twinkled, reflecting what was left of the sun. "Are you wavering, now?"

"M-maybe."

He chuckled, his hand warm, soft, firm on the back of her head as he brought their faces close. "All that I have, Winnie—all that I *am*—is yours. I *love* you. Fought it as hard as I could, but there 'tis—"

"But we've only known each other a few weeks," she said, anguish flooding her heart as she desperately tried to back up from the tide before she drowned. "And most of those we've been apart—"

"D'you love *me,* Winnie?"

"That's different," she said, watching the waters rise, helpless to get to dry ground.

"And how is that?"

"Because I *know* what I feel. I don't know what *you* feel. I hear what you're sayin', yeah, but—"

"You don't believe me?" he said, sounded a little anguished himself. When she didn't answer, he sighed, letting go. "You're *afraid* to believe me."

"Can you blame me?" she said to his profile. "And anyway, I'm the impulsive one, remember—?"

"Dammit, Winnie," Aidan said on a rough sigh, then swung his head back around to lance her with his gaze. "I'm only going t'say this once, and *only* to make a point." His mouth thinned. "I doubt I'd known June for ten minutes before I knew I wanted to spend the rest of my life with her. So it took me a few weeks with you—an eternity in comparison, doncha see?"

"Oh," Winnie said, catching on, but Aidan's finger shot up, stopping her.

"*But* since I've only been in love once before, I think it's fairly safe to say I'm not fickle. And I damn know what I feel. And as for your being impulsive…"

He was so impossibly gentle when he took her face in his hands, her eyes got watery all over again. "If y'hadn't made that snap decision to come see Robbie, I'd still be a miserable, lonely bastard convinced the best part of my life was over. But no, out you came to find your son, having no idea you'd be shaking me out of my coma, you daft, aggravating…oh, for the love of heaven!"

His mouth softly touched hers, tentative and earnest all at once, and the floodwaters rushed in, only instead of drowning her they buoyed her up into that safe, sweet place she'd nearly stopped believing existed. *But it does,* she thought, winding her arms around Aidan's neck and kissing him back. *It does, it does, it does….*

"D'you believe me now?" Aidan whispered, his own desperation a balm to an equally lonely woman's battered, tattered heart.

She smiled. "I'm working on it," she said, and he bent to kiss her again, but she said, "Hold on a sec, there's something I've been dying to do from the moment we met," and she lifted one hand to sift her fingers through his soft, silky curls. "Even better than I imagined," she said, and his smile was heaven.

They necked like a pair of teenagers for several minutes before, laughing, they came up for air to discover it was dark. On the outside, anyway. Inside was glowing like the damn Olympic flame. Judging from the grin she could barely see on Aidan's face, he was doing some pretty good internal glowing of his own. Then he wrapped her up tight in his arms, his chin resting on her hair.

"Okay, minor problem," she said. "E's daughter's kinda expectin' me to arrive tonight...."

"I'm sure she'll understand," he said, nuzzling her hair, and it occurred to her nobody other than Annabelle had ever really nuzzled her before. This was a decided improvement.

"And I still want to teach...what are you doing?"

He'd let go to extract a bunch of papers from his pocket, which he handed to her. "I know it's dark, so y'can't see them, but they're printouts of all the teachin' positions available in a fifty-mile radius. Including a third-grade opening at Robbie's school, come January."

Winnie clutched the papers to her, speechless. Aidan wrapped her up again and whispered, "Whether Robbie can ever find it in himself to call you his mother, I don't know—"

"That doesn't matter," Winnie said, jerking her head back. "I swear—"

"But I'd be beyond happy to call you my wife."

Her mouth hung open for several seconds until "What?" finally fell out of it.

Aidan smiled and started digging around again in his jacket, keeping one arm looped around her shoulders. "I even brought a ring. Just to prove how serious I am."

"What?" she said again.

"I hope you don't mind, it's not a diamond. But you didn't seem the diamond type. Of course, if you *want* a diamond—"

"No, I'm definitely…oh," she said on a breath when he tilted the smooth silver ring toward her, its large oval of finely veined turquoise gleaming softly in the moonlight. "Ohmigod, Aidan…it's gorgeous. I love it." She looked into his eyes. "I love *you,*" she said, swallowing when his eyes got all shiny.

"D'you think we could make a go of it, then?"

"I'm game if you are," she said, and he laughed.

"I'm no bargain, Winnie. I'm moody and messy and prone to being maudlin—"

"*You're* no bargain," she interjected, rolling her eyes, but he put his finger on her lips.

"But I also take the vow 'till death do us part' very seriously. I promise you, darlin'—I'll love you as long as you'll have me. If you'll have me a'tall, that is," he said, and in that instant she heard in his voice, and saw in his eyes—sort of, it really was getting pretty dark—all the *rest* of her wishes come true.

"You better believe I will," she said, holding out her hand, grinning like the world's biggest goofball when he slipped the ring on her finger.

"It fits perfectly," she said.

"So do you, darlin'. God help us both," he said, chuckling, neatly catching her mouth in another kiss before the squawk got completely out.

Winnie's friend Elektra—whose scream of joy at Winnie's announcement of their engagement gave obvious blessing to their impetuous decision—had begged them to stay the night at her house. However, knowing Winnie's desire to leave as soon as possible,

Aidan had insisted on driving back to Tierra Rosa that night. It wasn't until some hours later, however, when the dog and Robbie were both safely sound asleep on the backseat, that she said, "You do realize we just got engaged before we…you know. Geez…does anybody even do that nowadays?"

He glanced over. "Are y'thinking you'd like a free trial before you commit?"

She laughed, then said, "Actually…would you mind terribly if we waited until after the wedding?"

"Oh. Well, sure. As long as we're not talking a long engagement," he said, momentarily distracted by the erratic movements of a big rig up ahead. Then the bombshell hit. He stole another peek at the side of her face, his heart stretching at her expression. "D'you mean to tell me you haven't…? In nine *years?*"

"Hit the jackpot first time out," she said, grimacing. "Even though it took me a couple of months to figure it out. Right put me off, as you might say."

"But the boyfriends…?"

"Yeah, about that. Have one baby out of wedlock and every guy in town automatically assumes you're easy. Or desperate. Unfortunately for them, I'd made up my mind I'd never do…*that* again with anyone who wasn't ready and able to assume responsibility. And that didn't include just coming to the party with your dancing shoes." She sighed. "It was not, I soon discovered, a popular decision."

Aidan took one hand off the wheel to squeeze hers. "Some rebel you are."

"Not that I'm not interested," she said quickly. "Everything's in working order, believe me. But I'd done it just to do it and that definitely did *not* do it for me."

Aidan chuckled. "Nothin' like putting on the pressure."

"For heaven's sake, it's not rocket science," she said, and he laughed again.

"Maybe we should bypass Tierra Rosa altogether and go straight to Vegas?"

"Honey," she said, grinning, "if it wasn't for the kid and the dog, I'd take you up on that offer on a heartbeat."

Cooler heads prevailed, however. Long enough to hold out until Thanksgiving, at least, when they got married in their living room, with a handful of friends and family— including his parents, who fell under Winnie's spell far more quickly than Aidan—a half hour before a feast that Winnie herself helped cook.

Now, as the wedding party—full of goodwill and turkey—slumbered in various rooms of the house, Aidan hauled a shrieking-with-laughter Winnie into his arms to carry her over the threshold of the Old House, where some kind soul had already started a fire and made up the old log bed in soft sheets and a fluffy comforter. Winnie's cowboy boots—new ones, to go with her ankle-length, gold velvet dress with the hundred buttons running from neck to hem—thudded on the old, scuffed floor when he lowered her to it. His suede jacket ditched, he then tugged her over to sit on his lap on the rocker.

"Not exactly the piece of furniture I expected you to drag me to," she said, her smile soft in the firelight, her hands linked around his neck.

"I wanted to just…savor the moment," he said, skimming his thumb along her jaw, drinking in her fragrance and weight and rightness. "Isn't that what your mother taught you?"

"Yes," she said, tears glittering in her eyes. She kissed him, softly, then giggled. "Ohmigod…I'm *married.*"

"Surely you're not regrettin' it already?"

"It's really not a dream?" she whispered.

"It's really not. And twenty-four hours from now, you'll be in Ireland."

"Speaking of dreams," she said, then glanced around the room, frowning slightly.

"What is it?"

"I'm not sure. It's just…the house feels different. Than when I was first here, I mean."

"Different, how?"

"Lighter or something. Like a weight's been lifted. 'Course, that could be the champagne bubbles gone to my head, too."

Chuckling, Aidan whispered, "Come here," even as he felt the lightness, too, and he cupped the back of her neck to bring their mouths together, and then tongues got involved, and moaning, and not a little writhing, especially when he palmed her breast through her dress and thumbed her hard nipple and she practically leapt off his lap. *Good,* he thought, smiling as they kept kissing, and he started unbuttoning the front of her dress, and he thought she might have murmured, "Oh, yay, a multitasker." He smiled and pushed aside the dress's open front, nearly mad with anticipation, only instead of warm, smooth Winnie—

"What on *earth* are you wearing, y'daft woman?"

"Give me a break, I'm not used to it bein' this cold. And at least it's silk."

"At least. On your feet," he said, and she hopped off his lap, and he stood, as well, pushing the partially unbuttoned dress off her shoulders until it slithered to the floor, defeated, leaving his bride standing before him sheathed neck-to-toe in long underwear.

Not exactly how he'd pictured this moment.

Unbuttoning his own shirt, he nodded toward her. "Off with it. Now."

"Yes, sir," she said, wriggling out of the bottoms first, revealing the tiniest pair of panties, ever, then tugging the top over her head…and glory be, there they were.

"Oh, for pity's sake," she said, rolling her eyes. "They're just breasts."

"Now that's where you're wrong," Aidan said, and she laughed, and thirty seconds later they were naked and on the bed, each in his or her turn following the shadows of firelight on bare skin with their hands, their mouths, their breath.

"What d'you like?" he asked, nibbling, and she said, "How the hell should I know?" and he spread her legs, kissing his way down the inside of her thigh and murmuring, "Would you perhaps be thinking of the sampler menu?" and she said, "Uh, sure…except who's doin' the sampling? Not that I c-care," she said, when he kissed…

"Welcome to Funland," she murmured.

Aidan's head popped up. *"Funland?"*

"Yep. And you, buddy, just won a VIP pass for life."

He grinned, his heart—among other things—swelling with profound gratitude, that she'd listened to that voice or whatever it was a few weeks ago.

"Should I put on my dancing shoes?" he whispered, stroking her cheek, and Winnie smiled, that wonderful, exasperating, cheeky grin of hers that had bloody well saved his life.

"Not on my account. It's Barefoot Night in Funland."

"And you're goin' to drive that into the ground, aren't you?"

She laughed. "Sorry," she said, then lifted her knees. "Is now good for you?"

Hell, now was more than good, Aidan thought as he eased inside her, *now* was all that mattered…*now*, he vaguely thought as he whispered encouragement for her to relax so he wouldn't hurt her, was all a person had, wasn't it?

And a bit later, when his new wife sighed out a deeply satisfied, "Oh, yeah," the past quietly excused itself, leaving a profound sense of peace and blessing and joy in its place.

* * *

Thank you, Winnie thought, eyes closed, grinning like a Looney Tune, Aidan still inside her, still holding her. Still….there. That she wasn't even sure who she was thanking was of no consequence.

"So," he whispered in her ear, "was it worth the wait?"

Her laugh was lower, huskier, than she ever remembered it sounding before. She skimmed her fingers over his bare shoulder, then kissed it. "And I thought I couldn't walk after riding the horse."

Laughing, Aidan shifted his weight off her, his eyes dark and satisfied in the dancing firelight. With a trembling hand, he touched her cheek with the back of his knuckles, and she thought, *Oh, my Lord*…but that's about as far as she got. Then she giggled.

"Somebody's definitely not grumpy now."

"Not a'tall," he said, then released a breath. "Not anymore."

Winnie flipped onto her side to face him, smiling when his hand landed so naturally in the curve of her waist. The past three weeks had been about talking, mostly, yakking their fool heads off to each other about anything and everything, on long walks in the woods, on horseback, sometimes simply at the kitchen table until the wee hours of the morning. And laughing. Oh, my, yes, could this man make her laugh.

Make her feel like she'd finally come home. Now, her hands tucked underneath her cheek, Winnie said, "Warning…corn alert. But I really did see fireworks. Well, maybe not fireworks, more like…a single flash. Like…"

"Like a baby's laugh?" Aidan said, *completely* seriously.

"Yes," she whispered, then sucked in a breath. "Ohmigosh…you don't suppose…?"

"Robbie will be beside himself," Aidan said, grinning. Smug. Pleased as all get-out.

"Not to mention Annabelle," Winnie said, and he

chuckled and took her in his arms again, just to hold her. Then, slowly, her husband's hand, warm and strong and permanently paint-stained, dipped to palm her belly, and her eyes watered.

Because right now her cup wasn't half *anything*.

It was full to overflowing.

Epilogue

If you really put your mind to it, you might be able to make out the two blurry women playing cards at the bright white table, one in her late seventies with hair the color of a cock's comb, the other's hair long and silky, black streaked with silver. In life, they'd only met once; in death, they'd joined forces—the older woman, grudgingly—to do what some might call a little meddling. However, soon as this game's over, each will continue on her personal Journey, discovering whatever eternity has to teach her.

"I had no idea it would be so blamed hard," the older woman said, irritably. As usual. Those lessons she refused to learn in life weren't coming too easily on this side, either. "Although I don't see why I'm surprised—that granddaughter of mine's the stubbornest person to ever walk the planet. Just like her mother."

"Oh, come on, Ida," the younger woman said, discarding two cards and taking two more from the deck between them. Her mission accomplished, the vestiges of her corporeality were fading more with each passing second. "Admit it—don't you feel better?"

The older woman—still clinging to her body, even though the damn thing had failed her miserably for the last twenty years of her life—snorted. "Maybe." She'd assumed leaving her granddaughter everything she had in the world would have been sufficient atonement. She was beyond ticked to discover she'd been wrong. "You know, it's no picnic, suddenly finding yourself raisin' a child at the age I was. I did the best I could. Especially when Winnie came home—" she lowered her voice, even though there was no one to hear "—pregnant. And anyway, if I hadn't made her give up the child—"

"We wouldn't have had Robbie," June said, rearranging her cards. "It's okay. Everything worked out the way it was supposed to. Just as it always does."

You could hear the snort back on earth. "Like Bessie Jenkins getting my good Lenox?"

"Ida," June said, her smile peaceful. "You're dead, for God's sake. Let it go."

The old woman grumbled some more, then said, "I still don't get why you wanted them to get together."

June looked up from her very promising hand, wondering how it was that some people could have such a poor grasp on the obvious. "Robbie needed a mother. Since that couldn't be me, who better than the woman who'd given birth to him?"

"But to fix her up with your own husband?"

June felt the warmth of her own smile. "I've moved on. Why shouldn't he? The ceremony was lovely, by the way. You should've been there."

"I wasn't invited," Ida said irritably, and June realized the old woman was talking about the wedding, not the Day of the Dead vigil.

"I wasn't *there,* either. By that point, they didn't need outside help. Although…we knew there were no guarantees. We could set things in motion—"

"But no manipulating *e*motions, I know, I know." After a pause, the older woman added, "Guess that's the same everywhere."

"No. You can't make people love you."

"Sure is easy enough to make 'em hate you, though," Ida said, somewhat bitterly, and the younger woman thought she might have put her arm around her companion, if they'd still been alive.

Instead, she said, "Winnie's pregnant." At Ida's shocked gasp, June shrugged. "Seems even her eggs are impetuous."

"And that doesn't bother you?"

"Not at all."

Ida's mouth flattened as she tossed a nine of hearts into the pile, picked up another card. "Thought your only wish was to see *Robbie* happy again?"

"That wasn't going to happen until his father's heart was healed, too," she said tenderly, realizing that it would probably be another eon or so before Ida caught on to the concept of finding your own happiness in others'. But she supposed the old dear was getting there, one grumpy concession at a time. Still, after everything Aidan had gone through during June's illness, helping him over that particular hurdle was the least she could do….

June chuckled as the last card slipped into place.

"What've you got?"

She spread them out in front of the old lady, grinning.

"Full house," she said, and the old woman looked at her, her frown dissolving as comprehension began to dawn in her eyes….

* * * * *

The Colton family is back!
Enjoy a sneak preview of
COLTON'S SECRET SERVICE
by Marie Ferrarella,
part of
THE COLTONS: FAMILY FIRST *miniseries.*

Available from Silhouette Romantic Suspense
in September 2008.

He cautioned himself to be leery. He was human and he'd been conned before. But never by anyone nearly so attractive. Never by anyone he'd felt so attracted to.

In her defense, Nick supposed that Georgie could actually be telling him the truth. That she was a victim in all this. He had his people back in California checking her out, to make sure she was who she said she was and had, as she claimed, not even been near a computer but on the road these last few months that the threats had been made.

In the meantime, he was doing his own checking out. Up close and exceedingly personal. So personal he could feel his blood stirring.

It had been a long time since he'd thought of himself as anything other than a law enforcement agent of one type or other. But Georgeann Grady made him remember that beneath the oaths he had taken and his devotion to duty, there beat the heart of a man.

A man who'd been far too long without the touch of a woman.

He watched as the light from the fireplace caressed the outline of Georgie's small, trim, jean-clad body as she moved about the rustic living room that could have easily come off the set of a Hollywood Western. Except that it was genuine.

As genuine as she claimed to be?

Something inside of him hoped so.

He wasn't supposed to be taking sides. His only interest in being here was to guarantee Senator Joe Colton's safety as the latter continued to make his bid for the presidency. Everything else was supposed to be secondary, but, Nick had to silently admit, that was just a wee bit hard to remember right now.

Earlier, before she'd put her precocious handful of a daughter to bed, Georgie had fed his appetite by whipping up some kind of a delicious concoction out of the vegetables she'd pulled from her garden. Vegetables that, by all rights, should have been withered and dried. She'd mentioned that a friend came by on occasion to weed and tend it. Still, it surprised him that somehow she'd managed to make something mouthwatering out of it.

Almost as mouthwatering as she looked to him right at this moment.

Again, he was reminded of the appetite that hadn't been fed, hadn't been satisfied.

And wasn't going to be, Nick sternly told himself. At least not now. Maybe later, when things took on a more definite shape and all the questions in his head were answered to his satisfaction, there would be time to explore this feeling. This woman. But not now.

Damn it.

"Sorry about the lack of light," Georgie said, breaking into his train of thought as she turned around to face him. If she noticed the way he was looking at her, she gave no indication. "But I don't see a point in paying for electricity if I'm not going to be here. Besides, Emmie really enjoys camping out. She likes roughing it."

"And you?" Nick asked, moving closer to her, so close that a whisper would have trouble fitting in. "What do you like?"

The very breath stopped in Georgie's throat as she looked up at him.

"I think you've got a fair shot of guessing that one," she told him softly.

* * * * *

Be sure to look for
COLTON'S SECRET SERVICE
and the other following titles from
THE COLTONS: FAMILY FIRST miniseries:

RANCHER'S REDEMPTION
by Beth Cornelison
THE SHERIFF'S AMNESIAC BRIDE
by Linda Conrad
SOLDIER'S SECRET CHILD
by Caridad Piñeiro
BABY'S WATCH
by Justine Davis
A HERO OF HER OWN
by Carla Cassidy

SPECIAL EDITION

HEART OF STONE
by
DIANA PALMER

On sale September.

SAVE $1.⁰⁰ OFF

**the Silhouette Special Edition® novel
HEART OF STONE on sale
September 2008, when you purchase
2 Silhouette Special Edition® books.**

*Available wherever books are sold, including most
bookstores, supermarkets, drugstores and discount stores.*

Coupon expires December 31, 2008. Redeemable at participating
retail outlets in the U.S. only. Limit one coupon per customer.

5 65373 00076 2   (8100) 0 11556

SSECPNUS0808

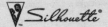

SPECIAL EDITION

HEART OF STONE
by
DIANA PALMER

On sale September.

SAVE $1.⁰⁰ OFF

**the Silhouette Special Edition® novel
HEART OF STONE on sale
September 2008, when you purchase
2 Silhouette Special Edition® books.**

*Available wherever books are sold, including most
bookstores, supermarkets, drugstores and discount stores.*

Coupon expires December 31, 2008. Redeemable at participating
retail outlets in Canada only. Limit one coupon per customer.

52608458

SSECPNCDN0808

REQUEST YOUR FREE BOOKS!

2 FREE NOVELS PLUS 2 FREE GIFTS!

Silhouette®

SPECIAL EDITION®

Life, Love and Family!

Silhouette Desire

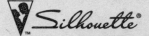

COMING NEXT MONTH

#1921 HEART OF STONE—Diana Palmer
Businessman rancher Boone Sinclair had it all—except for
Keely Walsh. But from the first time he saw her on his property,
he was determined not to let her get away…because every
Long, Tall Texan gets his way, and this one would not be denied!

#1922 THE RANCHER'S SURPRISE MARRIAGE
Susan Crosby
Back in Business
When her fiancé dumped her on the eve of their high-profile
wedding, movie star Maggie McShane needed to save major face.
Luckily, local rancher Tony Young agreed to a staged ceremony that
would rescue her image. But then their feelings became more than
mere Hollywood fantasy, and Tony rescued the starlet's heart as
well.…

#1923 HITCHED TO THE HORSEMAN—Stella Bagwell
Men of the West
After a stint in the air force and a string of bad-news breakups,
ranching heiress Mercedes Saddler headed back to her hometown a
little world-weary. That's when Gabe Trevino, the new horse trainer
on her family's ranch, gave her the boost she needed…and a real shot
at true love.

#1924 EXPECTING THE DOCTOR'S BABY
Teresa Southwick
Men of Mercy Medical
Management coach Samantha Ryan wanted unconditional love;
E.R. doc Mitch Tenney wanted no strings attached. A night of
passion gave them both more than they bargained for. Now what
would they do?

#1925 THE DADDY VERDICT—Karen Rose Smith
Dads in Progress
The day Sierra Girard broke the news that she was having district
attorney Ben Barclay's baby, he didn't know which end was up.
Commitment and trust just weren't his thing. But then a case he was
working on threatened Sierra's safety, and Ben realized he'd reached
a verdict—guilty of loving the mommy-to-be in the first degree!

#1926 THE BRIDESMAID'S TURN—Nicole Foster
The Brothers of Rancho Pintada
Just when architect Aria Charez had given up looking for Mr. Right,
Cruz Declan came to town. Visiting Rancho Pintada to meet his
long-lost father and brothers, the successful engineer was soon
overwhelmed by newfound family…until newfound love-of-his-life
Aria made it all worthwhile.